I0556188

BOUND IN BLOOD

MAGIC & MECHANICALS BOOK 3

JESSICA MARTING

SHADOW PRESS

Copyright © 2021 J.L. Turner

ISBN 978-1-989780-11-4

Cover art by German Creative

Edited by Christine Kirchoff

All rights reserved.

No part of this book may be reproduced in any form or by any electronic or mechanical means, including information storage and retrieval systems, without written permission from the author, except for the use of brief quotations in a book review.

CHAPTER 1

*D**ear Elora,*

I've grown weary of your complaints about funds. Going forward, I will be returning all correspondence sent to me from you, unread. Your inheritance from our parents should be more than sufficient to sustain the needs of a woman like yourself, and as such, you should have no need of an allowance from me.

As was the case with Uncle Frederick when he was still the duke, I am not obligated to provide for you.

I wish to enjoy my travels across Europe, and will not be communicating with you further. I suggest you find a husband.

Regards,

Peter Stone, Duke of Wexfield

ELORA STONE CAST a critical eye over her garret room, ensuring she was leaving nothing of importance behind. The last thing she wanted was for her landlady, Mrs.

Phillips, to find some precious thing Elora left behind and pawn it.

She shook her head a little at the notion. Elora owned nothing worth selling save the string of pearls that belonged to her mother, now resting securely in the satchel over her shoulder. There were only a few pearls left, the rest of the beads having been pawned by Elora herself, for such frivolities as lodging and food when her sewing income wasn't enough.

Something squeezed painfully at Elora's heart as she thought about how she would have to let go of yet another pearl from the necklace, this time to pay for passage out of London. She closed her eyes, as if to block out the sacrilege of selling off her mother's meager legacy, piece by piece, and waited until the guilt passed her by.

Hadn't Mother encouraged her to sell the necklace if Elora needed to? Wasn't she just fulfilling her mother's instructions?

When she opened her eyes, her room was just as it had been a moment ago: bare save for the narrow bed, rickety chest of drawers, and washstand provided by Mrs. Phillips. The attic floor's uneven boards didn't have so much as a rug to cover them. Just to be sure, Elora opened each drawer to check inside for any forgotten belongings, then under the mattress. She crouched on the floor to look under the bed and only saw some forgotten cobwebs.

A gray spider with spindly legs loped in her direction and Elora quickly staggered to her feet. *Not quite forgotten, I suppose.*

Satisfied that she had everything, Elora picked up her carpet bag, its handles worn smooth from use, and left the garret for the last time. Its door stuck in the frame as it always did, and she gave up trying to fight with it. What was the use? It wasn't as if she was coming back.

She descended the four flights of stairs to the rooming house's main floor, where she found Mrs. Phillips laughing with one of her favorite lodgers. Reginald Tavers lived in one of the best rooms on the second floor, and Elora suspected their widowed landlady had designs on him.

At the sight of Elora, Mrs. Phillips's good mood evaporated. "What's the problem today, Miss Stone?" she asked by way of greeting.

No hello? No how are you? Just irritation at the sight of her top floor tenant who had the audacity to complain about mice and spiders in her rented room. "Nothing today," Elora replied smoothly. "I've just come by to tell you that I'm vacating my room."

Mrs. Phillips blinked owlishly behind her oversized spectacles. "I beg your pardon?"

"I'm leaving," Elora repeated. "I paid my rent two days ago, and that's my last week's worth."

"But you haven't asked me for a reference," Mrs. Phillips said. "Why on earth would you want to leave?"

"I won't need a reference where I'm going," Elora said. "I'm leaving London."

"Wherever for?"

"That's none of your concern." Elora nodded at Mrs. Phillips and Mr. Tavers. She reached into her skirt pocket for the keys to her room and handed them to the surprised landlady. "Good day to both of you."

Without another word, Elora left the boarding house and strode into a scene of rare London sunshine. It was a beautiful spring day, and optimism soared through her veins for the first time in a very long while.

She may be the unwanted, disinherited sister of a newly minted duke, forced into a life of barely scraping by, but she finally had a future.

To access that future, all she had to do was rob her late

uncle and the previous duke's forgotten country home for its valuables.

That knowledge, combined with the spring sun hitting her face, bolstered her spirits as she walked to Boyle's Stock to sell another pearl from her mother's necklace. Unlike so many of Mr. Boyle's patrons, Elora was unashamed to be seen walking into the shop and even managed to smile at a pair of well-dressed ladies passing her by.

How could one be embarrassed to be seen entering that kind of place when she was so unnoticed to begin with?

The pawnbroker's shop wasn't busy on a Tuesday morning. Mr. Boyle, a slender, fair-haired man who balanced his wire-rimmed spectacles on the bridge of his nose, was always pleasant to Elora and never asked about the possibility of selling him her entire necklace. Elora supposed it would cost less money for him to conduct such a transaction, but she appreciated that he understood her situation.

"Good morning," she said cordially. She worked a pearl off her mother's necklace.

"Good morning to you, Miss Stone." Mr. Boyle pushed his spectacles up his nose, where they promptly slid down again. He picked up the pearl and examined it with a loup. "Is this from the same source as your other pearls?"

Elora nodded, although Mr. Boyle would already know the answer by now. He'd purchased six of them from her so far, all perfect specimens.

"Would you be looking to sell this today, or merely pawn it?" he asked.

Both of them knew the answer to that question, too, but he still asked it every time. "The money today, please."

"Of course." There wasn't a trace of judgment or condescension in the pawnbroker's voice, just a genial professionalism. She suspected he didn't care if his clients were working class or aristocrats, and judging by the wares in his shop, he served all kinds. Elora supposed that quality was important in his profession, and one that was probably lacking in the pawnshops serving the rookeries. Not for the first time, she was grateful that Mr. Boyle set up shop in a side street in her Hammersmith neighborhood.

Mr. Boyle wrote her a receipt and gave her the money, the same amount he'd offered for the other pearls Elora sold him. "Is there any chance of your ever selling me your complete set?" he asked.

It was the first time he'd brought up the subject. "I'm afraid not."

"Understandable. Although I'm sure you must know your pearls are exquisite. I've had buyers who would have loved to have the entire set it came from, if possible."

For a fleeting second, Elora considered Mr. Boyle's words. Selling off the rest of the pearls would provide her with funds that would last for months, if not a year or more. Her mother would have approved of the transaction, if it ensured her daughter's survival. However, she might grow complacent and back down from her decision to plunder her dead uncle's country house. There would be far better things to be found in that house to sell, items that weren't attached to memories.

"No, thank you," Elora said. "Just the single pearl today."

Mr. Boyle nodded. "As you wish."

EVENING HAD FALLEN by the time Elora finally found herself in Wand's Hollow at Thorn House, her late uncle's underused country estate. The mail coach she took was hot thanks to the crush of bodies squeezed into the conveyance, and it broke down halfway through the journey.

So, Elora waited at a nearby inn until a substitute carriage arrived in the mid-afternoon, and doled out some of her precious coins for a hot meal and a couple of roast beef sandwiches for her brief stay at Thorn House.

Very soon, she would have enough funds so she could afford whatever food she wanted. She would have enough to rent a nice flat or perhaps a seaside cottage, take a steam cab wherever she wanted to go, and buy clothes that fit her properly. Her secondhand dresses were always tight where they shouldn't be, or they nearly swallowed her barely five foot tall self.

The mail coach left her at Wand's Hollow's inn and postal office, and she walked the three miles distance to Thorn House. It was nearly fully dark as she trod along the dirt road, careful not to fall and twist her ankle in her slightly too-small boots. All traces of the spring warmth were gone, and she shivered in the darkness.

An owl hooted nearby, but Elora had no idea where it could be. She thought about the mice the owl was probably stalking for its supper and shivered.

Has the road to Thorn House always been this long? It was her first time visiting the manor in over ten years. The last time she and her brother had done so, they were taken there in a carriage. She and Peter were only twelve and fifteen at the time; he was already shaping up to be a horrible adult at that age.

Uncle Frederick ignored me the whole time we were there, and picked fights with Peter. Her uncle had never married, so he hadn't produced any heirs, which meant her brother would inherit the dukedom. Frederick considered Peter as nothing more than a useless, entitled wastrel, an opinion Elora shared, although Frederick was much the same. Few people, Elora included, wanted to be married to a wastrel, even if a potential fortune was on the table.

Although the last she'd heard of Peter's entitled ramblings, his new dukedom was hardly flush with funds. It appeared Frederick squandered his considerable wealth before he died in Scotland the previous winter.

She plodded on, guided by the full moon's bright light, keeping her focus straight ahead. Once in a while she thought she heard a twig snap behind her, as if someone was trying to be stealthy and failed, but when she whipped her head around, she didn't see anyone. It was probably a woodland critter, out for an evening stroll, or her imagination kicking into overdrive. She reminded herself that it was good to be paranoid. Keeping on her toes had kept her alive on more than one occasion as a woman supporting herself in London.

Thorn House finally appeared in her line of vision, a dark, brooding structure. It was smaller than she remembered, if not small for a ducal country house altogether, but Elora didn't care about that. The silverware would still be there, ready for her to take. If she was lucky, some jewelry might have been left behind, too.

She approached the front door, and in the darkness could still see the ivy creeping over the frame. The sight reached out to the romantic side of her that loved gothic novels, and was reassuring. No one had been in the house since well before Frederick died.

From her skirt pocket she removed a set of heavy brass keys. It was a spare set she'd stolen on her last visit ten years prior, hidden away in the same carpet bag she carried now. At the time, she played with them, then brought them with her when she and Peter returned home.

As an adult, they would make breaking in that much easier.

The pair of locks on the door groaned in protest when she turned the keys in them, but the mechanisms still gave way. The heavy door had swollen in its jamb, and she threw her shoulder against it to get it to move. On her third shove, she finally pushed the door in, and she stumbled into the pitch-dark foyer.

"Damn," she muttered. Shouldn't there be some moonlight coming through the windows?

She set down her carpet bag and fumbled through it for the flameless candle she knew to be in a pocket. Flicking it on, she cast it about the foyer, taking in the dusty surroundings. Outside, another owl hooted. Or perhaps it was the same one. Elora wasn't especially familiar with owls and their calls.

Some of her courage left her, followed by the strangest urge to flee.

Perhaps she should turn around, find an inn with lights and people, and wait until the morning to rob her dead uncle's country estate. "You've come this far," she whispered to herself. She cast the candle's light across the dusty floor. "You left your excuse for a home, you're all alone in the world, and you're about to take what's rightfully yours. Keep going."

Bolstered by the sound of her own voice, she forced her feet to move forward. She would find the least-dirty bedroom in the house and sleep there, she decided. Her stomach growled and she thought about the food she bought at the inn. *After I eat a sandwich, of course.*

Leaving her carpet bag in the foyer, she pressed on, guided by the flameless candle's light. It bounced off the walls with their peeling coverings, off the oil portraits of long-dead ancestors whose names Elora never bothered to learn. And it revealed footprints on the dusty floorboards where there wasn't any carpeting.

Elora froze.

Someone's been here.

A mixture of fear and fury welled up inside her at the revelation. *I had better be alone right now, and whoever was here had better not have taken the silver!* "Hello?" she called, hoping her voice sounded braver than she felt. Steeling herself, she approached the staircase and climbed it, her free hand gripping the balustrade. When there wasn't a response, she tried again. "Hello? Is there anyone here?"

She reached the landing, where the stairs split off in opposite directions. She went right, which would take her to the bedrooms. "If anyone is here, I must inform you you're trespassing," she said, exaggerating her London accent. "This is my home."

Something creaked from the direction of the bedrooms. Elora's blood ran cold.

Please be an exceptionally large mouse.

Something whispered over the floor, the rustle of fabric over carpet.

Please be an exceptionally large and well-dressed mouse.

Before Elora blinked, a tall figure appeared at the top of the stairs. It was too dark to make out any features, but it was definitely human-shaped. Man-shaped. The flame-less candle fell from her trembling fingers, but before it hit the stairs, she caught a glimpse of bright white teeth in the man's face.

Not teeth. Fangs.

An unearthly scream escaped her and her knees gave way. She fell backward down the stairs.

This is it. This is how I go. And Peter still gets to do whatever the hell he wants.

9

CHAPTER 2

*B*en moved faster than he ever did when he was alive, grabbing the fainting woman and breaking her fall before she could tumble down the stairs. His preternatural speed was improving.

It was too bad that she had breached his hideout. Unless he could glamour her and make her forget she had ever been here. Perhaps he would be better at that now. He crouched just enough to sling his arms around the backs of her knees and carried her downstairs. He spied a carpet bag in the foyer and wondered how she got here. What on earth was her mission?

She stirred in his arms. The smell of her hair and lemon verbena she'd dabbed on her pulse points reached his nose. Ben halted for a second, distracted. He'd loved lemon-flavored everything when he was still alive and this morsel smelled just like his favorite lemon tarts. His fangs, which had retracted after she fainted, extended again. He hadn't eaten a lemon tart since before he was turned. He hadn't realized until that moment how much he missed them.

Damn it. Now he would frighten her all over again when she awoke. Ben had enough difficulty trying to glamour someone when they weren't shaking in terror. This might prove impossible.

Not knowing where else to take her, he carried her up the rest of the stairs to the suite he'd claimed as his own at the end of the corridor. There was only one window in the bedroom, which he kept covered with a heavy drape, and he slumbered the days away in the room's canopied four-poster bed. Ben gently placed the woman on top of the covers. The scent of disturbed dust wafted around them and he realized the polite thing to do would have been to change the bedding before leaving her there.

It was too late to do that now. She was already stirring.

Ben quickly opened the drape to let some moonlight in the room, then lit an oil lamp on top of the washstand. He looked down at his clothes, noting with embarrassment that they were rumpled and disheveled. He hoped whoever she was wouldn't judge him too harshly for his appearance. His fangs were still out. *Damn it.* He willed them away.

Her eyes opened and she sat up in bed, disoriented. Almost immediately, her eyes latched on Ben. "What on earth?" she exclaimed, voice high-pitched in fright. She swung her legs over the side of the bed and stood up.

Ben deliberately remained rooted in place, not wanting to scare her any more than he already had. "Good evening," he said. He was as formal as would have been on a dance floor, waiting to take a turn with her about the room. Her blue eyes widened in surprise. For a second, he considered smiling to make himself appear less terrifying, but he wasn't sure that was possible when one's fangs made an appearance whenever they wanted to.

She looks as edible as she smells.

Oh, this was a terrible situation to be in.

A few unruly dark blond curls had escaped the bun at the nape of her neck in her fainting spell, and they quivered in time with her body as she regarded him. "Who are you?" she demanded.

He kept his gaze pinned on hers and hoped he could finally see into her mind. "No one you know," he said. *Oh, hell. She just blinked.* Once again, his attempt at glamouring someone sober had failed.

Confusion crossed her features for a few seconds. "Naturally," she replied. "What are you doing in my house?"

Now it was Ben's turn to feel fear grip him. "*Your* house?" he repeated.

If this was her house and she ordered him out of it… he would be powerless to stop her. He would be compelled to comply. It was one of the unfortunate realities of being a vampire, one of their few weaknesses. Even in death, vampires were subject to the near-supernatural whims of property owners and landladies.

She nodded, but he could still see her fright in the gesture. Something in him softened a little as he took her in: her threadbare, much-mended clothing, dusty from the day's journey. Her lack of jewels indicated her not being a fine lady. Ben was inclined to believe that she was the mistress of his hideout, if only because her attire was as shop-worn as the house.

But *she* wasn't. She was a bright flower in an untended, weedy garden.

"Yes," she said, but she didn't sound entirely sure of herself. "My house. You must leave at once."

Ben waited for his body to march out of the house against his will, but nothing happened. Some of the tension he'd been hanging on to since he heard her enter the place evaporated, and if was still alive, he would have sighed in relief.

This wasn't her house.

"Well?" she snapped when he didn't move. "Get out!"

"No."

She closed her eyes in frustration, and he guessed she was trying to figure out a way to get him to leave without any risk to her person. "You know, I don't care," she said when she opened her eyes. "Let me get what I came for, and you can destroy this whole beastly house when I'm gone."

Despite knowing nothing of the house's true owner, Ben felt a curious kinship with the place he'd made his home. It had been abandoned for years, which he suspected was the only reason he could stay. There wasn't a preternatural hold on the property that prevented him from entering without being invited.

"Wait," he said as she strode for the door. "You can't just come in and ransack this place."

Her eyes flashed at him in anger. "Oh? Have you already divested Thorn House of the silver?"

Was that the name of the property? Ben liked it. What he didn't like was the mention of silver. He hadn't known it was still possible, but goosebumps popped up along his skin. "Very well," he said.

"Very well, what?"

"Take the silver." He injected as much authority into his voice as he could. "Take *all* the silver. Take it away from this house."

"That was my intention."

Her gaze fixed on his, intense and suspicious, and for a second Ben forgot that he was supposed to be the one who could glamour people. He remained rooted to the floor, staring at her blue eyes until she turned away and left the room.

"Are you planning on killing me?" she asked over her shoulder.

Kill? Absolutely not. Such a delectable creature deserved to live and be admired. Would Ben care to sample her, see if she tasted as good as she smelled? He thought he might give his left fang for such an opportunity. "No," he said. He caught up to her as she reached the staircase, and she faced him, startled at his speed. At least that was one thing he'd mastered since he was turned.

"Who are you?"

He hesitated. "Ben."

"Ben what?"

Against his better judgment, he said, "Ben Lang."

"I've never heard of you." Gripping the banister with more force than necessary, she descended the stairs until she reached the landing, where her flameless candle still remained. Its light flickered on the faded carpet runner, correcting itself when she picked it up and held it upright. She held it in front of her, the soft light illuminating her features like she was a piece of art in a gallery. "Well, Ben Lang, what are you doing in my house?"

"This isn't your house. And it's polite to give your name when you ask for another's."

"It may as well be my house. It's in my family. And I don't know where you learned your etiquette, but officially, it's more polite to let someone else perform introductions." Her eyes narrowed. "And it's impolite to break into someone's ancestral country home and trespass for however long you've been here."

That explained why he wasn't forced away from the house. If a human occupant was away long enough, a vampire would be able to enter it at will. Ben had perused some of the papers and ledgers gathering dust in a study and knew the home belonged to a duke. "Are you the duke's daughter?"

"Oh. So, you *do* know who this house belongs to. And the duke was my uncle. He's dead now and the title's passed on to my worthless brother."

"That doesn't explain why you're here to steal the silver."

She actually rolled her eyes at that statement, marring the angelic look the candle under her face gave her. "It does. See, my uncle was a cruel and corrupt bastard, and no amount of his money could compel even the most desperate of ladies to marry him and sire heirs. So, when he died doing God knows what in Scotland last winter, the title fell on my brother, who isn't much better than Uncle Frederick. I've been completely ignored and disinherited since I was young, and I'm tired of struggling to get by."

Ben saw her situation clearly now. "And you're here to take what should have been yours, by rights."

"In a manner of speaking, yes. You wouldn't have stolen the silver already, would you?"

"No," he replied. "I have an allergy to it."

"Then you shouldn't mind if I help myself to it," she said. Finally, a smile appeared on her face. "I shall make a deal with you, Mr. Lang. You may stay here as long as you like, provided you don't interfere with my ransacking this place for anything of value. In return, you forget this visit ever happened." She turned away and started descending the stairs to the main floor.

"How do you know I haven't ransacked it already?" Once again, he swooped down the stairs to meet her where she was.

Her eyes widened in surprise. She clearly hadn't considered that possibility yet.

This close, their faces just a few inches apart, Ben could

see silvery flecks in her irises, the only kind of silver he wanted to be near at the moment.

"You would have taken what you wanted and left by now."

She had him there. He watched as she strode through the house, flameless candle held aloft as she navigated dusty corridors. She opened doors to rooms that Ben had never ventured into, poked around cabinets and along bookshelves, occasionally stuffing some trinket or other into her pockets. "Why are you following me?" she asked, without looking at him.

Because she was the first human Ben had spoken to since he was turned that he hadn't intended to feed from. Because she wasn't afraid of a strange man skulking around her family's country home and hadn't fainted dead away, well, fainted again, when he had his fangs extended.

She doesn't know I'm a vampire.

Something hadn't registered in her mind when she looked at him in his bedroom, or perhaps he had hidden his fangs better than he thought he had. But either way, she still thought she was dealing with a mortal man. She didn't look at him as she prowled through the room, but Ben knew she was expecting an answer. "You're the first person I've seen in a long time, is all," he finally said.

She brushed past him. He was helpless to follow her and her lemony scent. "Elora."

"I beg your pardon?"

Candle held aloft, she marched down a corridor to the formal dining room.

He easily kept up with her. "I beg your pardon?"

"My name is Elora Stone, Mr. Lang. Penniless orphaned sister of the Duke of Wexfield."

Once in the dining room, she sighed in irritation and threw open the draperies. Bright light from the moon and stars cast itself on the floor. Dust clouds rained down and Ben sneezed for the first time since he'd been turned. *Well, then. I had no idea that was still possible.* But the human response to dust wasn't what caught his attention. "Penniless?" he repeated. "How can that be, if you're the sister of a duke?"

She halted, incredulity written across her face. "Are you being serious? The upper classes eat their own all the time, which I'm certain you know about given the way you speak. I can tell that you've never mined coal a day in your life." Now it was her turn to sneeze. "And I already told you I was disinherited."

"You're correct in your guess about my station. But I still wasn't abandoned by my family. Nor am I closely related to any nobility."

"The mystery deepens, then." Elora opened a cabinet against the far wall and poked through it, holding her flameless candle above the contents. She gave a little cry of joy. "Here we are!"

Before Ben could reconsider, he crossed the room to see what she found so fascinating. "Here," Elora said, pulling things out of the cabinet. "Hang on to these for a minute while I get my bag." She dumped a pile of something shiny in his hands, the moonlight making the objects flash.

Not just anything. Silverware.

Ben immediately felt like an idiot. She'd told him, to his face, that she was here to steal the silver. Just as quickly, his feelings of idiocy evaporated, and pain radiated from his palms, up his wrists to his arms. It felt like a fiery serpent, aiming straight for the remains of his unbeating heart.

An unholy scream sounded through the house, followed by the crash of the cutlery against the floor. It took a moment for Ben to realize that the noise was coming from his own throat. He backed away involuntarily, some primitive vampire urge to survive taking over as he bolted for the opposite side of the room. The smell of burned flesh filled his nostrils. All through Ben's ordeal, Elora didn't move. But whether that was due to fright or shock or a combination of both, Ben was damned if he could tell.

Her gaze flicked from the pile of knives and forks at her feet to him, and back again. Finally, she fixed her eyes on him, still plastered against the wall.

His palms throbbed in agony.

Her words were slow, deliberate. "What the hell are you?"

CHAPTER 3

Terror had Elora rooted to the floor, the dropped silverware forgotten. The scent of burning flesh still hung in the air, and she was certain Ben's scream still echoed through the house. He had moved away from her and the cutlery faster than should be possible. Now that she'd seen it happen again, she knew her eyes hadn't played tricks on her when she fainted on the stairs.

The moonlight streaming into the dining room showed Ben in all his glory, including the fangs that she'd written off as imaginary, too. She surprised herself when she spoke. Her voice was strong and steady. "What the hell are you?"

Some of Ben's bravado dissipated. He touched his mouth, found his fangs there, and tried in vain to hide them. "Nothing."

"Oh, no. I don't believe you. Let me see your hands."

"What for? I have an allergy to silver. I merely forgot."

"How do you forget about an allergy that causes that kind of reaction?" Elora demanded. "And tell me what's wrong with your teeth."

"You're the first pretty girl I've seen in months. It was easy to forget."

Elora felt herself blush at the compliment and reminded herself that he was trying to distract her. "I'm not that kind of distraction. and you haven't answered my questions."

He finally peeled himself away from the wall and stalked toward her, his confidence clearly restored.

Run!

But she couldn't. Elora couldn't tell if it was due to bravado or plain stupidity. She didn't move as Ben walked back to where he stood before. He brushed aside the silver-ware on the floor with his shoe until they were face-to-face.

His fangs gleamed in the moonlight.

Oh, my God. He's a vampire.

She was in the presence of an honest-to-God supernatural creature.

"Elora," he said. His voice had taken on a darkly sensual edge that reminded her of velvet. It reminded her of luxury, of comfort, things that had been denied her for much of her life.

"Look at me," he continued.

Something in the timbre of his voice compelled her to do so, and she was nearly helpless to stop herself. The fantastical knowledge that Ben was a vampire slipped from her mind, as did the logical voice in the back of her mind that told her to get away from him, that he was dangerous.

"Elora?"

How did he do that? How could his voice sound so far away physically, but still resonate in her head?

When was the last time I caught the attention of a handsome gentleman?

Never, that was when. Elora was as invisible to other people as she was to what remained of her own family. She blinked, and just like that, Ben's voice's hold on her dissipated, like soap bubbles in an ewer of cold water on a winter morning. Was Ben even as handsome as she initially thought? It was too dark to tell by her flameless candle's light. She shook her head and took a few steps away from him. "What in God's name are you trying to do?" she demanded. "And I'll ask you again. What the hell are you?"

Ben was silent for a few seconds. Something in Elora told her this would be the best time to run, but she ignored the impulse again. For some bizarre reason, she wanted to hear the intruder's explanations, if he had any.

But he surprised her. "Damn it," he muttered.

"What?"

"I almost did it. That's the closest I've ever come to glamouring someone completely sober." His velvety voice turned angry, an emotion directed at only himself.

Elora understood that well. His words were the most concerning. "What do you mean, 'glamouring' someone?"

He closed the distance between them with that inhuman speed she'd noticed before, and his eyes fixed on hers again.

Elora didn't move, only holding the candle between them. His eyes really were lovely, she saw now. And he *was* a handsome man. His dark hair was slightly too long to be fashionable, but it suited him. A lock fell over one eye, and she fought the uncharacteristic urge to move it away, to see if it was as soft as it felt. His cheekbones stood out in sharp relief against her candle's light, as did the fangs protruding again from his mouth.

There they were again.

"God," whispered Elora.

"No," Ben replied. His voice had again taken on that

silky quality, and she felt it vibrating down her spine, spreading through her body. "Not God."

Dimly, the memory of the country house's crumbling stone chapel materialized in a shadowy corner of her mind. Would God reside in such a structure, on a property where His presence was never welcomed? "What are you?" she murmured.

His eyes were too dark to be human, the pupils gigantic. Ben leaned closer to her.

Elora's skin prickled with awareness, and she fought the urge to push herself against him, but just barely. An unfamiliar, but not unwelcome, impulse told her it would feel good, and asked her when the last time was that she'd been allowed to, or allowed herself, to experience that.

He moved aside a few strands of her hair until his mouth hovered by her ear and the sensitive spot under it. "I think you already know," he whispered. His lips slid over the delicate shell of her ear and down the side of her throat.

Did she? The scrape of his teeth, no, his *fangs*, against her pulse snapped Elora out of whatever daze she'd found herself in again, and she knew what he was. Her intuition was right. She pushed him away, but it was like trying to move a brick wall. She stumbled back and her bootheel caught on her skirt's hem, causing her to fall to the floor. God damn it, was she always going to be tripping over her feet around this man?

Vampire, she mentally corrected herself. Was she always going to be falling over her feet around this *vampire*?

Elora's knowledge of the creatures was slim. But she read a story in one of the penny papers long ago about bloodsuckers and their vulnerability to religious items and silver. Not being particularly religious, Elora didn't have a crucifix on her, but she'd just spent the last half hour or so ransacking her uncle's house for its valuables, some of which were only a few feet away. Quickly crawling on the floor on her hands and knees, she raced in the direction of the forgotten silverware. Reaching for it, she grabbed the first thing her hands touched, a teaspoon. She scrabbled to her feet, nearly tripping over her hem again in the process, and held out the spoon in her hand like a talisman.

Candlelight bounced off Ben's features. "Stay away from me," she said, hoping her tone carried more authority than she felt.

He didn't look alarmed to see the utensil.

For the first time in her life, she wished she followed the Anglican faith she was baptized in, that she had a crucifix on her person. Wasn't that what always repelled vampires in the cheap papers she enjoyed during her rare time off work? When she had a couple of precious spare hours to fret away and didn't want to think about her lot in life?

Ben remained rooted in place. He held up his hands, as if in defeat. "I'm not going to hurt you."

"Like hell you weren't!" Elora's exclaimed protest bounced off the walls. "You tried to eat me!"

He had the audacity to look sheepish. He rubbed the back of his neck with one hand in a silent admission of his guilt. "I wasn't going to eat you," he muttered. "I wasn't going to kill you."

"Is that supposed to make things all right?" She didn't take her eyes off Ben as she held the spoon and candle in front of her. She took a few cautious steps back to the spot where she dropped her bag. "What in the everloving hell did you mean to do?"

"I was trying to glamour you."

"Your fangs and teeth touched me," she snapped. The back of her foot hit her dropped bag, and she bent down to pick it up. She wished she had something more lethal than a silver spoon with which to defend herself.

"I'm not very good at glamouring humans. I'd hoped I was getting better at it, but…" He shrugged. "I wanted to make you forget you came here in the first place and smell you a little more before you left, is all."

"Those are all monstrous things to do."

"Fair point. I'm a monster, after all."

There was a note of sadness in his voice that pulled at her, and she hated it. He was probably only trying to manipulate her, and he'd piqued her curiosity. "How long?"

"How long what?"

"How long have you been a vampire?" She gripped the spoon, unwilling to release her hold on it even though Ben didn't appear alarmed at its sight.

"Uh." He scratched his head. "About a year."

Elora thought she misheard him. "I beg your pardon?"

"I was turned about a year ago," he repeated. "I was on my way home from a, well, the establishment itself doesn't matter to the story. Only that I ended up turned into this, and I don't think I'm very good at it." He ticked off his transgressions on his fingers. "I'm not very good at glamouring humans, I can't fly, I can't shift into a bat, and I'm a poor hunter."

Elora's stomach turned over, and her enraged indignation at his smelling her gave way to very real fear. The candle and spoon wavered in her shaking hands. She was in the presence of a killer, someone who would never be punished if he murdered her.

But a little voice in the back of her mind whispered to her, reminding her of her place in life. In society, or lack thereof. *If a human killed you, would he be punished? Would your own brother so much as lift a finger to summon a constable to investigate your death?*

Ben continued to talk. "I should clarify that I *have* glamoured a human a couple of times, but I'm unsure what I did correctly. At least they didn't remember my feeding from them."

Elora thought she might be sick. "You *fed* from people?"

"Of course," he said as if that bit of news was the most obvious in the world. And why wouldn't it be? The man was a vampire, for God's sake. "I didn't kill them," he added. "It's not that difficult to eat your fill and send your meal back home, or to the tavern he'd just stumbled out of to piss outside in an alleyway. Although now that I'm talking about it with you, I'm realizing how much easier it is to glamour someone who's already drunk."

He spoke about his abilities like they were nothing more than an unusual parlor trick, as interesting as a talent to wiggle one's ears for the amusement of others. "Oh, dear God." Was this her opportunity to run away and squire herself to safety? Was safety even possible? Ben claimed to be a bad vampire, but she knew firsthand just how quickly he could move. He would be on her in seconds. At least he'd mastered preternatural speed.

"Not in this house anymore, I'm afraid," Ben said.

If she didn't know any better, she would have thought he sounded wistful. "God never had a presence here," Elora said, hating the words as they escaped from her.

The mention of God reminded her of something important that had crossed her mind earlier. Thorn House had a chapel on the property, a long-disused stone structure that was built during George III's reign. Hope flared within her when she thought about it. Given that God hadn't played an important role in her late uncle's life, nor that of his father, little attention had been paid to the chapel's upkeep.

Just as quickly, the memory of herself playing alone in the chapel resurfaced, how she pretended it was a castle and she was its queen, the outside gardens full of her fairy subjects. Later, wanting to escape taunts from Uncle Frederick and Peter, she used the place as a refuge. She would bring her sketchbook and pencils or a novel to while away the hours drawing and reading.

I haven't drawn anything in so long. I used to be quite good at it.

What little energy she had in her time off hadn't been enough to summon the creativity and mental fortitude to complete a drawing or watercolor painting, to say nothing of the expenses of those items.

Why are you thinking about artwork now, you ninny?

She forced herself to focus on the manner at hand. She was in the presence of a real vampire, one who admitted to feeding off humans and she had to think of how she would ensure her own survival.

But is this a sign of the end? Was this an odd way of my life flashing before my eyes before I die?

"I'm not going to kill you," Ben repeated. "I won't even feed from you if you don't want me to. You can put down your spoon, take what you want from this house, and be on your way. I won't stop you." He hesitated for a few seconds before speaking again. "Since I can't seem to erase your memory of this encounter, I just ask that you not tell anyone that I'm here or that vampires are real."

His request was so unexpected and ridiculous that Elora nearly dropped her candle and spoon. She couldn't let it go without a retort. "Do you really think people would believe me if I told them vampires exist?"

"You're a duke's niece. You hold power."

"I'm a duke's sister, actually, and I have none." She

focused on what she said before, about how she could ransack the house and he would do nothing to stop her. "Do you give me your word that you won't harm me if I make my way through the estate?"

He nodded. "I may be a vampire, but I'm still a gentleman. I would advise you to stay the rest of the night here, though. I'm not the only vampire in the vicinity."

A cold chill tingled down Elora's spine as she remembered her walk to Thorn House after she alighted the mail coach. She had written off the sound of twigs snapping as belonging to wildlife, but hearing Ben tell her that Wand's Hollow was home to vampires… She shuddered. What if she had crossed paths with a vampire who was good at being one, instead of clumsy Ben?

The chapel had to be safest place for a human at Thorn House. "Ben, can you enter a church?"

Surprise lifted his dark eyebrows at the question. "I've never tried since I was turned. I'm not sure. Holy water doesn't agree with our dispositions."

That answered her question, sort of. She could quickly make the trip to the chapel and hide out there until morning, and then, by the light of day, she would raid the estate of everything of value that she could carry, and leave. She wouldn't fight Ben on his claim to Thorn House. If Peter ever bothered to haul his arse back to England and claim it, she was only too happy to leave him to the vampire's clutches.

Elora finally lowered the spoon and tossed it back in her bag. "All right," she said. "Let me get my things, and I'll find a place to stay the rest of the night." Catching his gaze in the flameless candle's light, she said, "You *do* sleep the day away, don't you?"

"Sadly, yes." There was a wistful note in his voice.

Elora had the impression that he missed the daylight. So did she, in that moment, for the safety it offered.

"That's more difficult to do than I thought it would be, so now I just go to sleep as soon as dawn breaks," he added.

But she didn't want to talk about the negative effects of the sun on a vampire. "If it's all right with you, I'm going to find somewhere to sleep. I've been traveling all day and didn't anticipate sharing Thorn House with anyone, let alone a vampire. I won't disturb you while you're sleeping in the morning. I promise." Without waiting for another word from him, and hoping her instincts that he wouldn't try to hurt her again were accurate, she turned around and walked away.

BEN WATCHED ELORA LEAVE, her flameless candle still held high as she marched purposefully through the house. His well-tuned hearing could follow her just as well as if he did so physically, and he listened to the gentle tap of her boots' thin soles against the dusty floors. She didn't stop and plunder anything else, which was troubling. What was she planning? Ben was familiar with Thorn House. There weren't any bedrooms on the main floor.

Was she fetching a stake?

Fear gripped at the empty place where his heart used to be. Ben had, by some miracle, mastered the art of moving silently through the house's corridors, a technique he'd practiced often enough since it was the only thing he was good at. He stole through them now, keeping a distance of a few feet from Elora's back. Silverware jangled in her carpet bag.

She defended herself with a spoon.

He hated that she was scared of him, and the spoon wouldn't do much damage if she tried to use it. But knowing him, he would probably trip at just the wrong moment and end up impaling himself in the eye on the damn thing.

She smells so good.

His vampiric senses were still in full swing. The scent of her hair and the lemon verbena she used as a fragrance perfumed the corridor. Beneath that, he swore he could smell her blood, heavy and rich. It reminded Ben that he hadn't had the chance to drink anything but animal blood for weeks.

She turned into the long-disused servants' kitchen.

Ben understood where she was headed. *She's going outside! After I told her not to, after I told her it isn't safe!* Elora Stone was going to be the death of him yet. His real death, anyway. He didn't stop her, not wanting to scare her again. So, he stayed close and waited until she slipped out the servant's door to the gardens.

Dread formed a hard ball in his stomach. Elora had been supremely lucky not to have been attacked this evening. While Ben hadn't met any since his arrival, he knew Wand's Hollow had attracted vampires as of late. He could sense others of his kind now, as surely as he could hear Elora's footsteps whisper over the grass.

Damn it, where could she possibly be going?

He let himself out of the servant's door, taking care to gently close it behind him so it wouldn't startle Elora. He still kept himself at a distance, cursing the full moon overhead that made both of them almost glow in its light. He fervently hoped she wouldn't turn around and see him. Ben moved slowly for fear of stepping on a twig and alerting her to his presence. Her walk was determined and overly confident. It was foolish after what Ben told her in the house about not leaving until morning.

I truly hope I don't have to get into a fight over her tonight. I don't know if I'll be in the same form I kept myself in when I was alive.

Elora stopped in front of a small stone building with a pointed roof. Its cross had long ago fallen off from its perch over the door, but Ben knew what the place was all the same.

A chapel.

She struggled with the door for a moment, its knocker banging against the swollen wood until she managed to dislodge it from its frame. She slipped inside and closed it behind her, the sound echoing across the property.

He didn't feel repelled, nor did twinges of pain radiate through his body as he approached the chapel, which likely meant any consecration or spiritual power the structure had had long since worn away. The only way Elora could have chosen worse for her hiding place was if she decided to sleep outside in the garden itself.

Ben sighed. Hunger pulled at him, rousing a primal urge to find some poor sod stumbling home from the village's only tavern and satiate himself. As he did every night, he ignored it and hoped a fox would cross his path.

Or Elora willingly would offer her neck to him.

He pushed that thought away. The notion of it sent every nerve in his body alight, and he couldn't afford to be distracted right now. He heard her rustling about in the abandoned chapel, and the occasional unladylike curse as a mouse skittered past her. He couldn't help but smile.

In life and undeath, he appreciated an assertive lady.

Ben sat down next to the chapel door, back against the wall, and kept his senses attuned to the world around him, ready to alert him to any vampires in Wand's Hollow before they could get to Elora.

CHAPTER 4

*M*uch to her disappointment, Elora didn't sleep. She hadn't expected deep sleep, but she'd hoped to doze off at least a little, to rest and build up her strength enough to face what was certain to be a bizarre day.

Vampires were real. She could scarcely believe it.

She lay awake, curled on her side on a hard wooden pew, and repeated the evening's events in her mind. Ben had tried to glamour her, and she didn't fully believe that he didn't intend to feed from her. And damned if she would have ever admitted to him that a small part of her was intrigued by the very notion.

It's because he's a vampire. They're supposed to be seductive.

Wasn't that what all the serials Elora read had said about vampires? Ben, while a bit clumsy and claiming to be a terrible vampire, was the most attractive man she'd ever met.

It was your candle that made his cheekbones appear as they did, you dolt.

But even as she told herself that, she knew it was a lie. His dark eyes had glittered like jewels by the sputtering light of her flameless candle, and she thought she could see the invitation there. Perhaps she was just seeing things. She was lonely and alone in the world, with almost nothing to her name save her late mother's pearls. She had never attracted attention from anyone before; there was something alluring and dangerous about catching the eye of a vampire. She shouldn't have liked it, but God help her, she did.

Speaking of God, would the chapel offer me enough protection?

The place must have been consecrated by a clergyman at some point, although that would have been decades, if not centuries before Elora was born. Its weather-beaten cross had fallen off from its spot over the door, and she hoped that didn't affect its safety. Did consecration wear off? Could the house's previous occupants be too depraved to keep the chapel's blessing effective? She had no one to ask but Ben, and her fascination with him aside, he was still a vampire. A *predator*. Although by his own admission, not a very good one.

Well, I'm stuck in quite the conundrum, aren't I?

She adjusted her carpet bag under her head that she'd been using as a makeshift pillow, and closed her eyes, hoping to will herself into drowsiness.

The chapel is so much creepier than I remembered.

When she'd cast her candle over the interior, she noted the rotting wooden pulpit at the front of the room. The tapestries depicting Biblical scenes installed on the walls were now water-stained and gave off the stink of mildew. The sashes over the windows, lovingly embroidered by a long-dead ancestor, were falling off their fastenings and moth-eaten. Had it always been in such disrepair, or had

Elora never noticed when she was a little girl? Her ruminations on the chapel's sad state were interrupted by a loud bang at the door. Elora bolted upright and swung her feet off the pew to the floor, heartbeat thundering.

"I've made a mistake," she whispered.

Hadn't Ben told her to stay inside? Hadn't he told her Wand's Hollow was dangerous at night? And then she'd gone marching away from the main house for the estate's rotting chapel. Any consecration of it was likely long ago worn away by the Stone family's appalling behavior.

Snarls sounded from outside, and there was another heavy thump at the door as if a body had been thrown against it. Elora froze, ears straining to hear more. Now she could make out scuffles, like a fight was taking place outside.

"Fuck off!" The voice sounded like Ben's but instead of the velvety, seductive tone he'd taken in the formal dining room, he sounded like he was in trouble.

"She's mine!" he said.

He's fighting for me!

Another growl, deep and almost animalistic, reverberated through the small space, making the hairs on Elora's arms stand on end.

"I can smell her!" exclaimed an unfamiliar male voice.

There was another thump against the door, and Ben cried out.

He was in trouble and on her account. Guilt tore through her, and she sprang to her feet, looking for something to use as a weapon. She couldn't believe she was doing this. *He's a vampire, for God's sake! He's a monster!* He'd stopped trying to feed from her when she asked, had he not? Did that count for something?

The table next to the pulpit holding an ancient cruet

33

set caught her eye. She ran for it, pushing the glass bottles empty of holy water to the floor, and turned the table on its side. One of its legs easily gave way and she snapped it off, hefting the wood in her hands.

This is madness.

Enraged howls outside sent chills down her spine, but she rallied herself and tiptoed to the door. She took a deep breath in a vain attempt to calm down, to make her hands stop trembling, before throwing back the door's bolt and opening it.

Ben was locked in a battle with a very naked man, who nearly glowed under the light of the full moon. Both of them had their fangs out, faces contorted in rage as they fought each other.

The action paused when Elora stepped in the chapel's threshold.

Her knees felt weak. The naked vampire's gaze caught hers and she tore hers away, looking at the patch of scrubby grass next to them, not knowing what to do next.

"She's smarter than I thought," he said.

From the corner of her eye, she saw him throw Ben aside as if he was nothing more than refuse, and rise to his feet. Despite the danger of the situation, Elora felt herself blush when she remembered that he was naked. He didn't rush at her as she thought he would.

She took a couple of steps back into the chapel, holding her makeshift stake in front of her like she did the spoon. In that instant, she realized that her broken table leg might be as useless as the cutlery. Would she even have the wherewithal to use it? Was the efficacy of stakes against vampires a lie from the penny papers?

I'm going to die and no one is going to notice I'm gone.

Rage and grief streaked through her, at the impending loss of her life before she had an opportunity to ever do anything meaningful with it. Rage at her brother and uncle, dukes who selfishly pushed aside their family members in favor of debauchery and depravity, who couldn't be bothered to so much as lift a finger to find a suitable husband for Elora, her only viable economic choice. At herself, for ignoring Ben, an actual vampire, and his warnings about other vampires in the area.

The naked vampire snarled again, spittle dripping from his fangs, then breathed deeply. "I thought I smelled a virgin," he hissed.

Elora shuddered in disgust. Oh, hell.

Chastity is a virtue, my fucking arse.

Any questions Elora might have had about a vampiric preference for virgins flew from her mind as she tried to process what was happening. For a few seconds, time seemed to stand still and silence reigned in the overgrown gardens, save for that damned owl's hooting somewhere nearby. Elora's heart beat so rapidly she thought Ben and the other vampire must be able to hear it. If anyone would be able to hear a heartbeat, it would be a vampire.

Finally, the naked vampire lunged for her. Elora screamed and her grip on her stake loosened. She gripped it again before it could fall to the floor, hardly noticing as splinters lodged themselves in her skin.

The vampire bounced off the threshold as if an invisible force held him back. Fury contorted his features, and he tried again. This time, he landed flat on his back, and before he could spring to his feet, Ben launched himself.

Inhuman snarls filled the air as the pair fought. Elora couldn't bring herself to move as she watched them, terror rooting her in place. The naked vampire roared and sank his teeth into Ben's arm. He pulled at his coat and flesh with a cruelty Elora hadn't known possible.

Ben faltered but pressed on. "She's mine!" Ben hissed.

Elora didn't want to know what that meant, but she did know that Ben was losing this fight. She looked at the table leg in her hand, now noting that it throbbed with the splinters, and knew she only had a couple of seconds to make a decision. Ben was trying to save her, undoubtedly for his own ends, but he wanted to keep her alive. The other one was all too excited to turn her into the vampire's version of a Sunday roast. She had to make it to dawn, and then she could be rid of this place. She had enough silverware to pawn for funds to take her at least to Scotland.

She would never make it out of Wand's Hollow if that vampire won in his fight.

Before she could talk herself out of it, Elora ran out of the chapel, brandishing her makeshift stake like the weapon of war it was in that moment. She didn't know the best place to stake a vampire, or even if it would work, but she had to try. She caught a flash of pale backside and focused on his spine as he snapped at Ben, now nearly pinned to the ground, and shoved the table leg into his back.

It was like drawing a knife through butter. The vampire froze, and a scream of agony and rage tore through Thorn House's grounds. His body started to disintegrate under the moonlight, chunks of gray flesh and red gore falling off his skeleton to the scrubby grass.

Ben pushed the body aside and got to his feet. By the time he was upright, even the skeleton lay in indistinguishable pieces. The stake wobbled in place for a few seconds, then fell to the ground.

Elora stared at the scene in horror. "Oh, my God," she whispered.

"Elora?" said Ben. There was a note of wonder in his voice. "I ... how can I ever thank you?"

She couldn't keep a sob from escaping her, and tears filled her eyes. "I killed him."

"He was already dead."

"I can't believe it," she said softly. She dragged a sleeve across her eyes. "I just killed someone. I—"

"*Elora.*"

She stepped back into the chapel. If the naked vampire hadn't been able to enter, she didn't see why Ben could, either. "No."

"Look at me."

"Fuck you." She hadn't uttered the epithet aloud in years, the last time being during her final conversation with Peter, but it felt appropriate.

"I'm not going to glamour you," he said.

She thought she could detect amusement in his voice, and it only made her angry. "Damn it, I'm trying to be nice to the person who saved my life tonight."

Against her better judgment, she looked at him. He stood a couple of inches outside the chapel, making no attempt to walk in.

"Unlife," he said, correcting himself. "You saved my unlife."

She had, and she remembered terror waving through her both of them. By his own admission, he was a bad vampire, and he'd tried earlier in the evening to warn her about the supernatural dangers that lurked in the night in Wand's Hollow. "I did it to save mine, too."

Lies. A part of her wanted the poor vampire to have a chance at making something of himself, whatever that meant for him. For the life of her, she couldn't figure out why that was a priority. He'd tried to glamour her, after all.

Ha. 'For the life of me.' It was better than the unlife of her, at least.

"I did warn you," Ben said, but there wasn't a trace of malice in his voice. Instead, there was an understanding, a human empathy, that Elora hadn't seen from him so far.

"You did," Elora replied. "And I suppose I was a fool for not listening to you."

"You did just learn about our existence. That's a lot to acknowledge in a short amount of time, in addition to losing your uncle."

The mention of Uncle Frederick reignited the old rage that had festered within her for years, pushing aside her terror. For a few seconds, she forgot about the greasy, bloody remains of the staked vampire piled outside the chapel. "He was a monster," Elora said curtly.

"So am I."

"Did you leave your orphaned niece and nephew to their own devices when they were fifteen and seventeen years old? Particularly the niece?"

Ben blinked, the whites of his eyes bright in the moonlight. "No," he said, disgust evident in his voice. "I have nieces and a nephew, or I had them when I was alive. I loved them to pieces. I still do."

Perhaps it was his dismay at learning how Elora had been treated growing up, or perhaps it was pity for him, but she didn't want to leave him alone in the night. A part of her was also tired of being alone, was desperate for companionship, even if the companion was a vampire. She moved aside, gesturing for him to enter the chapel. "Please come in."

He cautiously stepped over the threshold, probably half-expecting to bounce off an invisible barrier the way the dead vampire had. But he passed through as easily as Elora had.

"Why couldn't your friend walk in?" Elora asked, sitting down on a pew. Her hand throbbed, full of splinters, and she looked around the area until her gaze fixed on her flameless candle. She twisted the tiny key in the base until the flame burned high, and inspected her hand. She winced. It was going to be a pain digging them out.

Ben shrugged. "I'm unsure, but it could be because you, I don't know, imprinted on this place in a way that you didn't the main house. We can't enter the homes of the living without being invited. This must have been a special place for you."

"This was my favorite place when I was growing up," she admitted. "But I haven't visited in ten years."

Ben shrugged. "Perhaps the consecration effects on holy places wear off over time but not the sentimental effects." His voice softened. "I wish I could offer you more help."

Elora pulled a couple of splinters from her left hand and cringed at the discomfort as her nails dug into her skin. "But I'm your food. Why would you want to help me?"

"You're not just food. I'm not so far gone that I can't think of humans as anything but livestock."

The wistful note in his voice tugged at something inside her again, and if nothing else, provided a distraction from the vampire's remains congealing outside the chapel. Before she could stop herself, she asked, "Do you miss being human?"

His eyes widened in surprise at her question and sparkled by the light of the flameless candle. "I think if I was a better vampire, I might not miss it as much. There's something to be said for immortality and in imperviousness to all manners of lethal weapons."

The mention of weapons reminded Elora again of what was outside. "Except a leg from a church table."

"I can never thank you enough for that. I know it must

have been a shock, but you did a good thing tonight. Denis was out for us both."

"Was that his name?" *Why am I asking this? I don't want to know anything about the creature I killed! And of course, that's his name, Ben just used it!*

"Yes."

"Why did he come here?" She felt just as idiotic after speaking the words. She already knew the answer.

"Because you're food," Ben replied as if it wasn't a stupid question. "And you're particularly good-smelling food."

Elora cringed and hoped he didn't notice, but knew he probably would. "Because I'm a virgin." Was it just her imagination running amok on too little rest and too much stress, or did the tips of Ben's ears turn pink?

"That, too."

Elora pushed aside her embarrassment and forged ahead, wanting to know more details about her would-be murderer. "Why didn't you say anything earlier? Is that why you tried to eat me?"

"I didn't know. I wasn't familiar with virgins when I was alive and I'm not now. You smelled good on your own account. Like a lemon tart."

Her morbid curiosity and fear gave way to indignation. "Are you comparing me to pastries?"

"They were my favorite when I was alive. I hadn't real-ized how much I missed them until you let yourself into my house. And you're beautiful and brave and self-suffi-cient, and I don't see that often from humans or vampires."

A curious warmth spread through her at the compli-ments. She received them so rarely, and even coming from a vampire they were appreciated. But she couldn't keep herself from asking, "Was that because you haven't seen a human woman since you've been turned?"

"What?" he said, affronted.

"Did you think that because you haven't seen a human woman since you took up residence at Thorn House?"

"No!" he protested. "And I take deep offense to that question. Of course, I noticed you that way. I'm dead, not buried."

The last statement struck Elora as so ludicrous that she laughed, and for a few seconds she forgot about everything that had happened since she arrived in Wand's Hollow.

Except for the splinters in her hand. The throbbing brought her back to reality, and she remembered that they had to come out. She set her candle on the arm of the pew and studied her hand, the skin reddening around the tiny wooden pieces. With a sigh, she started working them out of her skin. Drops of bright red blood beaded on her palm and fingers.

She sneaked a glance at Ben, whose gaze was fixed to her hand. He wore the expression of a small boy looking in the window at a bakery, perhaps at a tray of lemon tarts. "I've just done something monumentally stupid," she said, not taking her eyes off him.

"You haven't," he said in an attempt to reassure her.

Elora still heard the longing and hunger in his voice, the tone of a person who hadn't eaten a proper meal in days.

"It's—well, I haven't seen or smelled anything that wasn't a fox or badger in a long time."

"You've been eating the local wildlife?"

He nodded.

"No humans?"

He shook his head. "I've fed from them before, but not in Wand's Hollow and I haven't killed anyone."

That was a pleasant surprise to hear. "You let your food go?"

He nodded again. "Always. I can glamour them enough after I've eaten so they won't remember. I've never drained anyone dry. I promise." His voice had taken on a rough quality.

His tone set every cell in her body aflame, and she felt herself blush again. She had never been desired before, and even though the cause of it was her blood, it affected her. She pulled out the last splinter from her index finger, and both of them watched as blood welled at the tip. "Do you promise now not to kill me?" She couldn't believe she was offering this. It wasn't just Ben and the way he looked at her. Now she was curious how it would feel to be fed on by a vampire.

His breath caught. "What are you offering?" There was cautious hope in his voice, a wary excitement.

Elora felt the same rising in her. She held out her hand, a fine tremble to it. "A lemon tart."

Was she making the stupidest mistake of her evening that was already marked by stupid mistakes?

Ben took her hand in his, but instead of diving in, fangs extended, the way she guessed he would, he looked at it like it was something precious that he was afraid to break. He lifted it to his mouth and licked at her bleeding finger.

Elora's breath stuttered. His hands and tongue were cooler than she was, but she couldn't tell if it was because he was a vampire or because she felt like she was on fire. Her clothes, already a little ill-fitting, felt too constrictive like she needed to get out of them to feel normal. The notion of getting naked with Ben sounded very right.

He sucked her fingertip into his mouth.

A small cry escaped her and she clapped her free hand over her mouth to muffle it. Ben groaned, the sound sending vibrations up her arm. His teeth and fangs scraped against her skin. Elora stiffened, unsure whether to be alarmed or to continue feeling aroused. But Ben didn't come at her neck with his fangs, instead keeping his focus on her finger, which had to have stopped bleeding by now.

A bolt of unfamiliar, but welcome heat shot through her when his eyes met hers, and she couldn't have torn her gaze away from him even if she wanted to. A logical voice at the back of her mind told her to look away before he glamoured her and sank his fangs into her throat, but she ignored it. She slowly blinked, if only to reassure herself that she was still in charge of her body's reactions, and a dimly lit part of herself was grateful for that.

Abruptly, Ben ended the contact, nearly flinging her hand away from him.

A different kind of hurt threaded itself into her, more painful than the splinters in her hand. When she looked at Ben, she saw his fangs were extended and his pupils nearly black by the light of her flameless candle.

He stood up. "We should go back to the main house. It isn't safe here," he said brusquely.

"Of course, it is," Elora said. Her clothes still felt too tight and her body protested at the broken contact from him. "No one can come in here unless I invite him."

"You could be glamoured into inviting a vampire in. I can keep you safe at the main house until dawn."

"But vampires don't have to be invited into the main house," Elora protested. She shuddered, again forcing the image of the dead creature from her mind. "They could just let yourselves in there and they can't with the chapel. I'm staying here. That table has three other legs I can use to defend myself."

"Elora," Ben said, and she stilled.

Can vampires glamour humans with just their voices? Why does he have to sound so damned sensual?

"I would never forgive myself if something happened to you on my account," Ben continued. "I doubt Denis was the only other vampire in the vicinity. We'll return to the house, you can get some rest while I keep watch, and then you can be on your way in the morning."

It sounded so reasonable, and yet… "What about you?" she asked.

"What about me?"

"What if a vampire comes after you because you stole Denis's lemon tart virgin?"

"I will handle that when it comes to that. I think it would be best if you took the first mail coach out of here back to London. When you return, stay inside at night."

A chill slithered down Elora's spine. London was already dangerous enough without supernatural elements. "All right. Let's go back to the house." She reached for her bag, but Ben picked it up faster than she thought possible and slung it over his left shoulder. He offered his right arm to Elora, the picture of a gentleman save for the fangs extended over his bottom lip. She didn't ask why they were still out. She wasn't sure she wanted to know.

She took his arm, and let him escort her back to the house as if they were nothing more than a courting couple returning home from a midnight gala.

If Ben's heart still worked, it would have been beating so loudly as to be audible to his lovely companion. As it was, he trembled like a young lad on his way to a brothel for the first time, but if Elora noticed, she didn't let on.

She was trembling, too, but probably due to fear more than nervousness.

I've been nothing but a nervous wreck since I was turned. What's the use in immortality if I can't enjoy it? He was afraid of other vampires, afraid of humans finding out what he was and staking him, afraid of the sun.

Elora was none of those things. She'd been frightened of Denis, but she reacted and saved both of them.

And she let him *taste* her.

He replayed that memory over and over in his mind, how he savored the few drops of blood she offered him. How he had to force himself away from her before he lost control and killed her. He hadn't killed anyone yet when he fed from them, but he had a few close calls. Humans were so fragile. *I don't know whether I want to eat her or fuck her.* The crude thought popped into his mind and refused to go away. *Or both.*

"Ben?"

He tamped down the quandary plaguing him. "Yes?"

"Is it true vampires can't tolerate the sun?"

He hesitated. A great deal of what was being published in the cheap penny papers, all the horrible vampire serials, was disturbingly accurate. Some of it was exaggerated. It would take more than a piece of cutlery or silver jewelry to harm a vampire but other legends were true. Particularly that of sunlight's effects on the undead. Was she planning on killing him? Throwing open the curtains of the bedroom he'd claimed for himself as dawn broke?

He was more attracted to her than any other woman since he'd been turned, maybe even before, but he couldn't tell if she felt the same. He chose his words carefully. "It doesn't agree with us."

"Do you have somewhere safe to sleep? I can't imagine the curtains in Uncle Frederick's old bedroom are heavy enough to keep the sunlight out. There's a root cellar that would be a better hiding place. I'll show it to you when we get back."

Ben thought about his dead heart, how if it could, it would have skipped a beat. A proper daytime hiding spot had been elusive to him since he fled London

Oh, Elora. I hope you decide to stay with me forever.

CHAPTER 5

*T*he safety of daylight beckoned Elora through a crack in the drapes and she blinked, grateful for the sun.

I lived through the night.

She didn't have to contemplate if the events of the night before were nothing but a dream, because she woke up in Uncle Frederick's bedroom, in the bed Ben used since he decided to take Thorn House for his own. She stood up and stretched, her joints and muscles aching, another reminder of everything that had happened since she arrived in Wand's Hollow.

Oh, my God. There's a dead vampire outside the chapel.

Nausea roiled in her belly. She would have to take care of Denis's remains this morning. *How the hell am I going to do that?*

She answered herself just as quickly. *Just bury him, you dullard. There's an old gamekeeper's cottage on the grounds that's bound to have at least one shovel.*

Elora wondered for a moment if she should check on

Ben in his new hiding spot in the cellar, then quickly dismissed the notion. She didn't like being woken up from a deep sleep; why the hell would a vampire appreciate that? And it wasn't as if she was in danger of dying should sunlight hit her face.

I wonder what it would've been like if we'd slept in the same bed.

She felt herself blush, and then remembered how he'd sucked the blood from her fingers last night, how oddly exciting it was. A part of her wanted him to do that again. "It must have been all the upset," she whispered to herself as she dressed. "I was just so relieved to be alive after that vampire tried to kill me that I couldn't help but feel that way." Even as she said the words aloud, trying to convince herself, she knew them to be untrue.

It's entirely because of Ben and how he touched me.

It was a gesture that would have reviled her not ten minutes before it occurred. It ended up being something that Elora mulled over and over in her mind as she tried to fall asleep. It would be a memory she would treasure forever. She fiercely wished it could have led to something more.

But it didn't, she reminded herself. *And he's a* vampire. *You're his food source.*

According to Denis, she was a delicacy. Elora's face burned when she remembered how he'd sniffed the air around her, his terrifying delight in announcing she was a virgin. It wasn't something she'd ever thought about before, and she assumed no one else would think about it, either, let alone bring it up in conversation. Did it count as conversation when one of the people involved was trying to eat the other? She supposed it didn't matter. Denis was dead, and Elora was leaving Wand's Hollow forever.

She prowled through the bedrooms, grabbing jewelry

pieces from long-dead ancestors that now gathered dust in drawers. There wasn't as much as she initially thought. But she still ended up in the possession of several gaudy brooches crammed with rubies and sapphires, and a set of pearls that included an ugly tiara. Elora wondered who had once worn the awful thing and was grateful to whoever had such terrible but expensive taste. A collection of diamond stickpins, the gems of varying sizes, was also taken, as were a few pairs of gold and silver cufflinks. The metal was a little tarnished, but it was nothing that affected the pieces' monetary value.

Elora's bag was considerably heavier than when she arrived. The purloined silverware clanged even though she'd wrapped the cutlery in a silk scarf. All of it was her ticket to a new life, far away from London. She thought about a cottage at the seaside, with a vegetable garden and perhaps a dog or cat to keep her company. It was a reminder that everything that had happened since her arrival at Thorn House would be worth it.

Her stomach growled at the foot of the stairs, and she remembered she hadn't eaten since she had supper at the mail coach inn. "Sandwiches," she murmured. "I still have two." She dug through her coat pockets for the wax paper-wrapped beef sandwiches she bought at the inn. They were a little misshapen, but still edible. Elora tore into them like an animal, or possibly a vampire with a human throat exposed in front of him.

She was glad Ben wasn't there to watch her make a pig of herself.

Once her breakfast was demolished, she remembered the final task she had to do before she left Wand's Hollow on the next mail coach, the whole point of her early excursion.

I have to bury Denis.

Dread threaded its way through her and her cold breakfast threatened to come back up. She still forced herself to walk out of the house, through the overgrown gardens and lawns to the chapel. Sunlight cast itself on the ground, making the old structure look almost romantic, the kind of place where lovers might meet for a tryst.

She remembered the look on Ben's face as he licked her blood off her finger as they sat on a pew, the roughness of his voice as he commanded she follow him back to the main house.

Maybe she imagined it. She'd been without attention from anyone for so long, particularly male attention, that she was projecting her own unmet desires on a vampire she'd just met. She didn't know which part of that revelation was most disturbing.

Her curiosity, rather than disgust was roused in her when she approached the chapel's door, a shovel in hand that she'd found in the abandoned gamekeeper's cottage. Instead of a bloodied mess of bones and sinew with a broken table leg sticking out from it, all she found was a pile of pale grease. Her makeshift stake rested on the ground next to it. "What the hell?" Elora said aloud. She poked at the grease with her booted toe, felt it squish beneath her sole.

The substance didn't look like a corpse. It wasn't even body-shaped. As Elora watched it, she thought she could see it drying up in the rising sunlight, turning into dust. She couldn't bury dust, so she dug up the ground around Denis's remains and tossed some earth and weeds into what he used to be. She'd been granted a boon, she thought as she returned the shovel to the gamekeeper's cottage. Hopefully, her string of good luck would continue when she left Wand's Hollow.

IT WAS mid-morning when Elora returned to the village's train station. Sunlight streamed over the old building, a relic from another time before dirigibles were invented. Although Elora doubted there would be much demand for air travel among Wand's Hollow's residents, who, according to Uncle Frederick, never left the town unless it was in the back of a hearse.

Come to think of it, one of the reasons her uncle spurned Thorn House was because of the lack of dirigible accommodation. Uncle Frederick owned a black dirigible all to himself, an ostentatious beast he was far too proud of. Elora hadn't seen it in years, but she assumed Peter took possession of it when he inherited the dukedom. She had never been aboard one. Air travel was out of the question when one lived hand to mouth in London.

An ornithopter waited in front of the train station, its passenger basket empty and wings lowered. Elora adjusted her bag's strap over her shoulder as she took in the small flying machine. Wand's Hollow might not have the infrastructure in place to accommodate a dirigible, but an ornithopter was another thing altogether. Its wings were finished with blue and green enamel, a pattern that reminded Elora of a dragonfly. Its wicker-sided basket looked new, brass fastenings polished.

The ornithopter was a curious sight, but she didn't have time to dawdle over it. She opened the door to the train station and was immediately greeted with the stench of death. Not for the first time that morning, her stomach heaved, but she kept her breakfast down.

"Stop!" a man's voice commanded. "Don't move another inch!"

Elora remained rooted in the doorway and blinked, trying to make sense of the scene before her. The building's windows were small and set just under the ceiling, which didn't allow for much morning sunlight to stream through. The gas lamps hadn't been switched on, leaving the foyer dark. Clusters of flameless candles were set up instead, their tiny artificial fires giving the area a funereal atmosphere.

Except it wasn't the candles doing all the work. That was performed courtesy of the dead man lying on the polished wooden floor or rather, what was left of him. He lay on his back in a pool of dark congealed blood, shirt collar ripped away to reveal the chewed-up remains of his throat. His eyes were open and wide with terror, mouth agape in a silent scream.

It had to have been a vampire.

Denis had done this. She remembered the dark stains around his mouth and caked to his chin that reminded her of wine. Any guilt she harbored over staking him evaporated. Elora couldn't help it. She screamed and backed out of the train station. She looked around frantically for somewhere to run, but couldn't force her feet to move.

Footsteps thundered along the floor until a man, a live one, stood before her. "Pardon me," he said. He touched Elora's arm. "I apologize. I should have locked the door, but I'm looking for evidence right now and it slipped my mind."

Elora jerked away, unable to handle human contact at the moment. "Who was that?" she asked, voice quavering.

The man's tone softened, and his next words were spoken kindly. "That was the postmaster. He took care of the train station and sold tickets. Did you know him?"

Elora shook her head. "No. I'm only visiting. I was

going to buy a ticket for the next train back to London." She couldn't keep tears from leaking from her eyes and she wiped them away impatiently. She'd seen enough death for one lifetime, in less than the space of a day.

"May I ask you some questions?" he asked gently. "Just about if you've seen any suspicious activity since you've arrived in Wand's Hollow?"

Elora stiffened. The last thing she wanted to talk about was every bizarre thing that happened when she came to town to rob her family's country home. "Who are you?"

"Sergeant Merritt Sloan. I work with the Liverpool City Police."

A feeling Elora didn't recognize welled up inside her. It was a strange and frightening combination of fear, relief, and distrust.

It was good to see another human in Wand's Hollow, of which she hadn't since she alighted from the mail coach the day before when the postmaster greeted her with a nod. That man's desecrated body was now lying in a pool of his own blood.

But something the policeman said bothered her. *Liverpool?* Why was a Liverpool police officer investigating a murder of an unknown rural postmaster in a village fifty miles from his city? The nearest large town, Tillsbury, had a modest constabulary that could have investigated the postmaster's murder.

Sergeant Sloan could be lying about his position, but what could be gained from that?

Her questions aside, Elora nearly blurted out how she'd killed a vampire the night before, and she'd already solved the mystery of the murderer. But then she would have to bring the sergeant back to Thorn House. She would have to explain her burglary and the vampire slumbering the day away in the cellar. Not to mention Denis's desiccated remains that were probably still rapidly rotting away to nothing. She would be arrested for theft and murder and hanged by the end of the week. Or she would be committed to a madhouse by the end of the day.

Sergeant Sloan's expression was unreadable, but Elora knew he wanted answers.

"I came to town last night to visit my late uncle's home," she said. That much was the truth. "He passed away last winter and my brother inherited his dukedom. My brother's out of the country at the moment."

He removed a pencil and a small notepad from his coat pocket and scribbled a few notes. He quickly steered the conversation back to Elora and Wand's Hollow. "Is this Thorn House you're speaking of?"

She nodded, and that sick feeling returned to the pit of her stomach. "How did you know that?"

"I had a chance to read about some prominent residences in the area before I arrived," Sergeant Sloan replied. "Thorn House has been unused for quite some time, hasn't it?"

Was she walking into a trap? Elora chose her words carefully. "It is. I wanted to conduct an inventory of the unentailed items in the house."

"I was given the impression that Thorn House is a private property and not entailed at all to the dukedom."

Blast it all, how did he know that? Elora shrugged, hoping the gesture came off as authentic. "I'm doing what my brother asked me to do, is all. Anyway, I couldn't get into the main house." Her mind worked quickly, trying to figure out plausible excuses as to why. "The locks on the doors are rusted shut. My keys didn't work."

"You said you arrived last night. Where did you spend the night, if you couldn't get into the house?"

"There's a chapel on the property that was open. I did have to force the door to get in. I hope that isn't illegal." Her gaze drifted to the open door and she noticed how abruptly the light cut off in the foyer. She couldn't see the dead postmaster from this vantage, but she felt his presence like a curse all the same.

"Well, no," said the sergeant.

Elora forced herself to look at him, to seem as sincere and honest as possible. His blue eyes were crinkled at the corners, but she suspected the wrinkles weren't from a life of laughter. He didn't look much older than her twenty-two years, but he had a haunted look about him that gave him a gravitas beyond his age. He had the face of a man who had seen a lot of death.

"It's only illegal if you broke the locks on the door," Sergeant Sloan added.

Elora shook her head, probably with too much enthusiasm. The motion caused a faint clank of silverware in her bag. The sergeant raised his eyebrows at the noise but didn't comment on it.

"You haven't told me your name."

"Oh. I suppose I haven't. It's Elora Stone."

"I noticed there isn't a 'lady' in there."

"I'm not one," she explained. "Our fathers were brothers. Uncle Frederick didn't marry, so he didn't have any direct heirs. Peter became duke after our uncle passed."

"And you said that was last winter?"

She nodded. "In Scotland. We don't know what he was doing there, but he died in a small barony in the highlands."

Sergeant Sloan had been writing everything down that she told him, but his pencil stopped at the mention of Uncle Frederick's last whereabouts. "Do you know anything about that?"

Elora shrugged and hoped she wouldn't dislodge any more of her stolen property. "We haven't had any contact in years. He wasn't one to support me after my parents died."

"Did your brother or husband?" His pencil resumed scribbling, and he flipped the notebook's pages to a fresh one.

"No, and I don't have a husband." She tried to speak the words as if it didn't matter, but it did. It wasn't just the financial and social benefits marriage brought women, but companionship, too. She'd been alone for most of her life, and she was tired of it.

So, she tried to bring the conversation to a close. "I couldn't get into the main house, so I spent the night in the chapel and now I just want to get back to London. As dismissive as this may be to mention it give the circumstances, but is there any other way to buy a train ticket today? Mail coach or third class on a passenger train?"

"Ah." Sergeant Sloan's pencil stopped moving again. "Well, no."

Elora thought about the dead body in the train station and shuddered. "I hate to ask, but could you go in there and bring me a train schedule?" she asked. "Perhaps I can buy a ticket on the train itself, considering the circumstances. I think a mail coach passes by in the mornings here."

"There won't be trains stopping here for a while," the sergeant replied. "They've been rerouted pending an investigation." He squinted at her as if trying to ascertain if Elora was real or not. "Did you see *anything* suspicious last night?"

Sweat popped up along her brow and she fought the urge to wipe it away. She hadn't been arrested, and she hadn't done anything illegal, not really. She was the sister of Thorn House's owner and had every right to be on the property, whether she broke in or not. She was also positive it wasn't illegal to kill a vampire since they weren't known to officially exist. "How long will the trains be rerouted?" she asked. "When can I leave?"

"Did you see anything suspicious last night?"

Damn it, she'd forgotten to answer that question. "No," she said, perhaps a little too quickly. "Although I haven't visited Wand's Hollow in many years. I suppose the definition of 'suspicious' has changed since I was last here."

"Did you speak with Mr. Goode last night?"

Elora cocked her head. "I beg your pardon?"

"The dead man."

"Oh." A shudder rippled through her. "No. I saw him last night but we didn't speak before I walked to Thorn House. As you can see, there aren't a great deal of vehicles to be hired here."

"I did notice that," Sergeant Sloan replied. "That's why I brought my own." He inclined his head at the ornithopter.

This seemed an appropriate time to say something polite about the man's conveyance. "It's very nice."

It was the right thing to say. "Thank you." He smiled at her, and some of the years on his face fell away.

For a moment, she wondered why he became a sergeant with the Liverpool City Police. The thought of the police reminded her of another question. "You haven't told me why you would come all the way from Liverpool when there's a perfectly competent constabulary in Tillsbury."

"Ah," said Sergeant Sloan.

Was it Elora's imagination, or did his cheeks turn pink? She kept her expression as inscrutable as possible, not wanting the sergeant to think she knew anything about the murder. It would make his job a great deal easier if she could just tell him the killer was already dead, but he wouldn't believe her. It would be best to encourage him to leave Wand's Hollow, for at least as long as it took her to get away.

"That constabulary has been notified," Sloan finally said. "They've already made their investigation."

"How? It's not even eleven in the morning."

"The postmaster's son found him earlier today and immediately sent for the constabulary. They sent me a telegram, and here I am."

"You? Not all of Liverpool's officers?"

"I'm best suited for this kind of work. I have the experience to conduct a more thorough investigation and a faster mode of transport."

Realization dawned on Elora. "I see. You aren't here on behalf of the Liverpool police. You're here because you're curious."

"I'm an investigator," Sloan said, voice sharp.

"You're doing a favor for someone."

"Constabularies and police forces will do that for one another, yes, but that isn't my motivation today. Now, did you see anything suspicious last night?"

"I already told you, no." Frustration welled up in Elora as surely as blood formed on a finger after a splinter was removed. "When do you suppose the trains will start running again?"

"Not for a few days."

"Is there any way for me to get out of Wand's Hollow until then?"

"I'm afraid not, unless you can convince a local to escort you. The postmaster's son will be taking over his father's duties when he's able to." Sadness fell over Sloan's features. "Poor lad. He's had the worst fright a person can get. He's not even twenty yet."

That meant the younger Mr. Goode loved his father, which almost certainly meant his father loved his son. Jealousy flared in her, bright and hot, for a few seconds as she wished she'd had that kind of relationship with her own father or brother. "I'll be on my way, in that case," Elora said. She sighed.

"Where will you go?"

"Where do you think?" she snapped. "I have to go back to Thorn House." When Sloan opened his mouth to protest, she held up her hand to silence him. "It's daylight now, Sergeant. I'll be able to find my way around rusted locks with my keys in the day better than in the dead of night after a day of travel. I'll just have to sort out some food until the train starts running again." She inclined her head at the sergeant, the lone black-dyed feather in her hat drooping dangerously low over the brim. The stupid thing probably needed to be sewn back in place again. She turned around to head back without offering another word to Sloan.

"If I have any more questions for you, will I find you at Thorn House?"

Elora stilled, and she faced Sloan again. She did not want him digging around her uncle's house, and he seemed the type. A strange protectiveness washed over her when she thought of Ben, hiding away from the sunlight in the cellar. Weirdly, he was depending on her right now. Ben wasn't the monster who had torn the poor postmaster's throat out. He didn't even enjoy being a vampire. He ate foxes, for God's sake.

"Only until the train service starts again," she said, her voice calm. It hadn't wavered a bit to reveal her unease. "Although I'm sure you'll understand that I won't want to answer the door to a man I don't know, even if he is a policeman. Good day, sir." She nodded again. "I hope you find Mr. Goode's murderer."

She could feel the sergeant's eyes boring into her back as she walked away, but she didn't turn around, for fear her suspicions were confirmed.

CHAPTER 6

One of the only human characteristics Ben maintained after he was turned was the ability to slowly wake up and stretch, with an accompanying optimism that the promise of a new day brought. Except for today, when his eyes opened in a disused coal cellar, dark as pitch. The coal was long gone, but he could still detect an old aroma of it, dank and thick. He usually didn't rise feeling especially hopeful. When he woke up when he was still alive, he was usually feeling the effects of a night about town, with too much imbibing and too much cavorting with women whose names he never remembered.

Tonight, his internal clock told him that it was past sundown. His vampiric senses could hear Elora Stone shuffling around the house upstairs and she was cooking something, judging by the scent that reached him in the coal cellar. Was she the reason for his optimism tonight? Because she hadn't returned to London? Why the hell hadn't she run away from Wand's Hollow as fast as her legs could carry her? There was only one way to find out.

Ben dressed, sniffing his clothes beforehand and cringing

at the scent of coal clinging to the fabric. It wasn't as if Elora hadn't already seen him in a poor state. He made his way out of the cellar to the kitchen, taking care to make noise so as not to startle her. Although, he mused as he fussed with his shirt collar, he wouldn't say no to her falling in his arms again. It would be far more preferable if she did it because she wanted to, not because she was about to fall down the stairs.

His tactic worked.

He found her stirring something fragrant in a large, dented pot over the fireplace in the kitchen. Dark blond curls had slipped from the knot at the base of her neck and fell around her forehead in a way that shouldn't have been as adorable as it was. She'd unbuttoned her blouse's top buttons in a futile attempt to cool off, if the humidity in the air was any indication. "Good evening."

"Is that your way of saying 'good morning'?"

She nodded and removed her spoon from the pot. She tasted whatever was on it and considered the taste for a second. Then she put the spoon back in and stirred. "Yes."

"Why are you still here?"

"Getting right to the heart of the matter, are we?" Before he could respond, she barked out a short, harsh laugh. "Huh. Heart. I guess you would want to get to it."

"I've never eaten a heart. That's just disgusting."

"I think Denis might have tried last night." She unhooked the enormous pot from its hook over the fire and set it on the cracked stone floor. She took a seat at a table that would've been used by servants once upon a time, and which Ben noticed was now wiped clean.

He pulled out a chair and sat next to her. "You killed him," Ben pointed out.

"Yes, but when I tried to board a train back to London, I found out that the postmaster was murdered last night. A

Liverpool policeman was investigating this morning." She massaged her temples as if to rub away her troubles. "I saw the body."

Ben felt his insides turn queasy, a feeling he hadn't had since before he was turned. "I'm sorry you had to see that."

She shook her head a little, and a tear slid down her cheek. "He had his throat ripped out," she said softly. "Maybe more than that, I didn't get a good look. And I didn't want to."

Ben remembered how Denis looked last night with the bloody stains around his mouth and chin, the scent of viscera clinging to him. Ben had dearly hoped the older vampire had just tucked into a poor fox in an especially brutal way, but he'd known, deep down, that all of the blood on him was human. Denis had always been off-kilter and violent. Ben had heard that vampires tended to embrace their worst traits, their darker sides, the older they got and the further away from their humanity they drifted. It was a fear of his.

What would happen to him in five years? Fifty?

Five hundred?

How old had Denis been? Ben had heard him mention his skulking about Versailles and later the guillotines during the French Revolution. He described the bloodbaths and beheadings with glee.

"It could have been Denis," Ben said.

"I hope it was," Elora replied. She sniffled. "I don't think I could handle knowing another vampire is about."

But they were. Ben could feel them. Wand's Hollow was a tiny hamlet, but it was a tiny hamlet on a well-traveled train route. He knew vampires who still preferred to travel that way if they couldn't fly or shift into bat form. Not all

63

of them could. Ben hadn't mastered it yet. "I hope it was Denis, too," Ben said, trying to reassure her.

"Anyway, they've stopped the trains until the postmaster's murder is solved. However long that will be. And I still don't know why a sergeant from Liverpool is here when there's a closer constabulary in Tillsbury, but he is."

Ben was worried about the policeman. If he stumbled on a vampire or a vampire nest, he stood a good chance of being killed. A big city sergeant's brutal murder would bring more big city sergeants descending on Wand's Hollow like a plague. "All right. You'll stay here until it's safe to leave."

"You say that as if you have any authority over this house."

"Neither of us does, legally but please listen to me when I ask you to stay inside this house at night. Don't wander over to the chapel. Stay here, with me."

"How do I know you won't try to eat me again?"

"I give you my word as I did last night and I will again. I'm not so far gone that I can't keep a promise to not feed from a human, if it will make her feel safer."

Elora rose, and inspected the heavy pot. "I'm too hungry to wait any longer for this. Do you want some? It's chicken soup."

"I would if I could, but I'll have to decline."

She took a clean bowl from a cupboard and ladled some soup into it before taking her place at the table. "It's miserable offerings," she said, poking her spoon around the bowl. "I had to make do with what's available in the village market, and there isn't much. I bought a chicken, some sad vegetables, and a loaf of bread that's been kept alive longer than it should have. They'll have to do for now."

"Are you out of money?"

Her spoon hovered over the bowl, steam issuing from

it. "Not quite, but I do need to get back to London and pawn what I can."

"And then what?" He enjoyed the turn the conversation had taken. It felt much longer than a year since he'd last had such a chat. Come to think of it… it had definitely been longer than a year. He hadn't sat down at a table that wasn't for cards and shared a meal with someone since before he left home.

She shrugged and swallowed her soup. Still too hot, she made a face but didn't say anything about it. "Buy a cottage at the seaside, I suppose. A place like Wand's Hollow but isn't Wand's Hollow. Just an out of the way spot, where I could keep a vegetable garden and raise chickens, perhaps a goat." She scooped up soup and blew away the steam. "I would've saved the chicken blood for you, if I could."

"I beg your pardon?"

"The chicken blood," she repeated as if he was simple. "It was already butchered when I bought it. If it was a little… fresher, I suppose, I would have asked the butcher to save it, so you could have something tonight, too."

Ben was touched that she'd thought to do such a thing. He hadn't expected that kindness. "I appreciate the intention. Thank you."

She ate more before she spoke again. When she did, her voice was soft. "Did you mean it when you told me last night that you've never killed anyone?"

"Yes," he said emphatically. "I swear to you. I've fed from humans, but I don't do it often."

"How often are you supposed to?"

It was on the tip of his tongue to offer a sharp retort, something like, *How often are* you *supposed to eat?* But he stopped himself in time. She was the closest thing he'd had to a friend since he was turned, and besides that, he liked her, very much. And not as a delicacy. "Regularly. I make do with foxes, but it isn't the same." Her blood last night had been his first human blood in months and just the taste had nearly led to his undoing.

"Did you hurt the people you fed from?"

"No, and I like to think I'm gentle."

"You put your fangs in people's necks. How could you possibly be gentle?"

"I managed and I can usually glamour humans into forgetting it happened, remember. And, well." He cleared his throat, an uncharacteristic wave of shyness washing over him. "Humans often find it pleasurable."

Color rose in her cheeks as understanding dawned. "Oh." She stirred her soup before asking another question. "How did you end up a vampire? If you don't mind my asking."

"I had the impression that you would ask anyway."

"Is it rude to ask?"

"I'm not all that familiar with vampire etiquette to tell you," he admitted. "I came here about four months ago and hadn't spoken with another vampire until Denis arrived. They pass through here and I can sense them, but they leave me be." He adjusted his shirt cuffs, again feeling shy. "I was turned just over a year ago when I was walking home from a…" He fumbled with his next words, part of him not wanting to appear as the utter cad he had been in life in front of her, the other wanting to be honest.

Because he now considered her a friend. Because she deserved honesty.

"A brothel," he said. "I was walking home from a brothel in West London, and I didn't feel like spending the last few pennies in my possession for a steam cab or hack."

She didn't seem fazed by his admission. "Was it Madame Tremblay's?"

He hadn't expected that response. "How do you know of that place?"

"My brother made it his mission to fuck everything in skirts from one end of the city to the other when he was still in London," she said. "He also ran into trouble with Madame Tremblay when he was late settling his accounts more than once. It must have been three or four years ago, before he turned me out."

Surprise had Ben pinned to his chair, and he didn't know what shocked him more. Elora was familiar with the brothels of the upper classes, she used the word 'fuck' in that context, and her own brother had pushed his sister out of his life. She'd spoken of him before when she was ransacking the dining room of its tarnished silverware, but of course, there hadn't been enough time to ask her about him further. That was what he decided to focus on. "Why would your brother abandon you?"

Elora shook her head. "Oh, no. You're not getting out of telling me how you came to be a vampire." She ate the last spoonfuls of soup, scraping the bottom of the bowl.

"I actually wasn't avoiding the topic. For all my bad behavior when I was alive, I didn't desert my family, and I didn't have a wife to be unfaithful to or children to disappoint."

"What were you?" she asked.

"Human."

She gave him a withering look. "I know. What I mean, what were you? I can tell from your speech you're from a good part of London. You already admitted you were a patron at Madame Tremblay's, and her house's services aren't cheap. Were you the heir to something?"

"I'm the fourth son in a family that made its fortunes in industry, in flying machines and watches. My mother's family factory produces propellers and engine components.

My father's timepieces. I'm not mechanically inclined and there was no need for me to become that way, so I was free to do as I pleased."

"You were a spoiled brat," Elora surmised.

"I wouldn't go that far. I didn't demand special treatment."

"You broke into my family's country home and claimed it for your own. That sounds like something a brat would do."

"Desperation breeds that kind of behavior," Ben said, trying not to be irritated. "It was better than staying in London, surrounded by all those delicious people, eating them, and leaving them in the Thames to terrify the masses."

Her eyes widened a little at his statement, but she didn't argue.

Instead, he noticed how the light from the fire made her eyes sparkle and brought out warm reddish notes in her hair. The sight was enough to make him forget about the cloying heat in the kitchen. Well, almost forget. The heat made her hair fall out of its style, a look she likely hadn't intended but was nonetheless alluring.

"Would you really have lost control if you stayed?" Elora asked softly.

"I don't know. Possibly, if I came across some poor soul lying in an alley, bleeding out after he was robbed."

"Was Denis... normal? For a vampire?"

Ben thought of what he knew of the vampire, what a sadist he had been. "I believe vampires embrace the worst of themselves as they get older," he said, choosing his words carefully. "Denis certainly did, and so did a number of vampires I knew when I was still in London. I think the most long-lived of us tend to be crueler. They embrace it. The ones I've known enjoyed being vampires and felt superior to humans. They'll also do anything to survive."

"You said 'they.'"

"What of it?"

"'They'll' do anything to survive," Elora repeated. "Not 'we will' do anything to survive. You don't think you're one of them. I think that's really why you came here."

That idea had hovered in the back of Ben's mind since he first stowed away aboard a Glasgow-bound dirigible departing from Vauxhall Airfield. The dirigible had been flying low enough for him to see the endless fields and moors, interspersed with villages. He'd picked Wand's Hollow at random and let himself fall from the dirigible, landing in an undignified heap not two feet from the wooden fence posts surrounding Thorn House.

She got up again without waiting for a response from him and started cleaning up the kitchen.

The soup was ladled into bowls and arranged in an icebox in the corner, which Ben noticed was freshly stocked with ice. He could smell it, and for a few seconds, he desperately craved a glass of cold water. "Why did your brother leave you?" he asked, changing the subject. "Where were your parents?"

"Dead. Our father when we were small children, and our mother nine years ago. I always suspected Uncle Frederick had something to do with Father's death, but of course, I couldn't prove it."

"What happened?"

"He fell down a flight of stairs," she replied. "Specifically, the stairs at Uncle Frederick's town house in London. Their childhood home. Father was cut off when our uncle inherited the dukedom. He went there to ask for a small loan to pay for school books and a tutor for Peter. We never saw him again. Since our father was liked by everyone in their circle and our uncle was a jealous, spiteful thing, we thought he was murdered."

"I'm sorry. That's terrible."

Elora gave a small half-shrug, trying to be nonchalant, but Ben saw through the gesture to the pain and regret beneath. "I can't prove it but I wouldn't have put it past Uncle Frederick." She collected her dishes and set them in a sink with a water pump. It was an ungainly, stiff thing, probably designed by someone who wanted the servants to suffer while trying to do the simplest of chores. Elora struggled with it, barely pushing the handle down.

"Let me," Ben said. Before she could protest, he nudged her out of the way. He rolled up his shirtsleeves and set to work. He felt the pump give under his strength. Cold water flowed into the sink, a light reddish-brown at first, before it flowed clear.

"Thank you," Elora said. She picked up a rag and cake of soap. "I can take over from here."

"Do you want help?"

She looked at him like he'd grown two heads. "Are you serious?"

"Yes."

She narrowed her eyes at him. "Men of your station don't clean dishes."

"I'm not a man," he reminded her.

"I beg to differ."

He caught her gaze and held it. He wasn't doing it as a vampire with the intent to glamour her, but to see what she meant. "I'm sorry?"

"You can be both and you are." She handed him a small towel. "You can dry."

～

THERE WAS something appealing about taking Ben by surprise, Elora mused as she finished washing her dishes. She didn't even care that the water was freezing cold as she soaped up her rag. What was the discomfort of a little cold water when she could make a vampire blush? Because she was *sure* Ben was doing that right now.

A vampire who could still blush couldn't be *that* dead.

Then there were his forearms. Dishwashing marked the first time she'd seen them, and his rolled-up sleeves revealed a lean strength that his being dead hadn't diminished at all. Elora surprised both of them when she pointed out that he was still a man. She felt herself flush when she thought of how he was caught off-guard, an almost heady feeling.

It evaporated when she remembered the dead postmaster and how she couldn't leave Wand's Hollow. Sergeant Sloan said the trains being rerouted would only be a day or two, but she wouldn't be surprised if it was longer. Even when the trains were allowed to stop in Wand's Hollow again, the policeman might still be investigating the postmaster's murder. Sergeant Sloan had made a special trip just to look at bloody footprints, or whatever policemen did when they investigated killings, all the way from Liverpool, the only policeman to do so.

He was here because he wanted to be.

The memory of Sergeant Sloan was at the forefront of her mind, next to Ben and his forearms. As much as she would have loved to keep thinking about Ben, the policeman had to be discussed. "How many humans know about vampires?"

Ben was putting dried dishes away, opening cupboards and cabinets willy-nilly to find their spots. He paused. "I haven't a clue. None of the ones I've eaten from. I made sure of that."

"You never heard rumors when you were still with your vampire friends, never saw humans with them?"

He considered her words as he put away her soup bowl. "Some vampires have human familiars. The vampire who turned me told me about a couple she knew, although she didn't have respect for the practice. Most vampires look down on our kin who mate with humans."

"Why? It seems convenient to have a food source and friend in one."

"It would be," Ben replied. "But would you want to keep a cow as a companion?"

"Of course not," Elora replied. Ben reached for the silverware she used, rag in hand, and Elora swatted it away. "And I know what comparison you're trying to make, and it doesn't work," she continued as she dried the spoon and ladle. "Cows and humans are both food, but vampires used to be human. Still *are* human, just with different abilities and aversions." He had an odd, unreadable look on his face when she glanced at him after she put away the silverware. "Ben? Are you all right?"

He collected himself. "Yes. Thank you."

"For what?"

"A lot of things. Not being afraid of me. Staking Denis, even though I know how frightening and upsetting that was. And you came back."

The last words were spoken wistfully, and she realized just how lonely he had been.

"You didn't have to return here. There's an inn, not too far from Wand's Hollow that you could have stayed at until train service resumes."

Part of her wanted to tell him that one of the reasons she returned to Thorn House was because she had a measure of guaranteed safety with Ben, since he knew vampire culture. She also wasn't sure she could afford an indefinite stay at an inn, no matter how dilapidated and cheap it would surely be in this part of the country. "I could have," she said slowly, mulling over what her limited options would have been. "But coming here made the most sense to me."

"You have no ownership of the house."

"I have, with the chapel and…" She wasn't sure how to put her thoughts into words without sounding like an empty-headed ninny or calf-eyed schoolgirl. "I felt bad, leaving you here alone. I don't know why." Something shifted in his expression, like he'd just exhaled after holding his breath. She wasn't sure if he could still breathe. Then his face broke out into a grin, and she felt a corresponding warmth in her heart at the sight. "I shouldn't be fond of someone who wants to eat me like Sunday dinner but God help me, I am." The mention of a deity reminded her of something she wanted to ask him. "Will the mention of God bother you?"

He shook his head. "I don't think so. I believe it's the faith of the person holding holy objects or names that gives them their power, but I've never been in a position where I've had to find out. I've avoided holy water just to be sure. The chapel didn't bother me."

"Thorn House was a place of poor morals long before you ever crossed its threshold."

He nodded. "An unloved and uninhabited place of poor morals."

"And silver?"

"It would take more than a spoon to hold me off. Silver bullets or chains are more significant." He spoke with her freely now, and the conversation was fascinating.

"Can you drink? I mean, can you drink wine? I'm sure there's a bottle of something around here, and I could use a drink."

"I don't know. I could try." He sounded so hopeful.

"Did you like wine when you were still alive?"

"Who doesn't?" He chuckled to himself. "Although I had a great many pastimes I had to give up when I was turned."

He followed Elora out of the kitchen to the dining room, where she hunted along dusty shelves for wine that had to be there. Uncle Frederick always took care to leave wine in every one of his homes, for any possible occasion. She found an unopened bottle beneath the sideboard, near the cabinet she'd liberated of its silverware, but no glasses. Instead, she fetched a pair of teacups. "I wonder what happened to the crystal," she said, realizing for the first time that it was all gone.

"Perhaps someone got to it before you."

"Or Uncle Frederick had it removed to his town house in London. It doesn't matter. I wouldn't be able to get it to a pawnshop without it breaking." She opened the wine with a knife stabbed through the cork and poured cupfuls for each of them.

Ben stared at his with longing before gingerly picking it up and inhaling over the contents.

The sight was fascinating enough that Elora set aside her own cup and watched him. It was like witnessing a small child staring longingly at a bakery window, and she was reminded that he told her she smelled like lemon tarts.

He must miss food. *Real* food. He took a sip and set the cup down in its saucer.

"How was it?" Elora asked.

"Delicious, but I don't want to have any more until I can be sure it won't make me sick."

She nodded and took a drink. Even her unsophisticated palate could tell the wine wasn't great. Uncle Frederick would have kept his best bottles at his London residence but it was drinkable. Time hadn't destroyed it. "How do vampires get sick?" she mused aloud.

"Much the same way humans do. Although I haven't gone out of my way to test out how. I was told I couldn't eat human food after I was turned. No human food, no sunlight, no wooden stakes."

"Did you fall on stakes a great deal when you were still alive?" Something warm sparkled in his eyes at her quip, and she liked the feeling the sight gave her.

"No."

"What about garlic?"

"Are you going to try to kill me via lasagna?"

"No," Elora said. "I want to know how much about vampires is true, compared to what I've read in the papers."

He regarded her thoughtfully under his dark sweep of lashes. "I never would have taken you for someone who enjoys the dreck in the penny dreadfuls."

"They're in my budget. Novels aren't. They aren't as bloody and gory as I like my adventure stories to be. You didn't answer my question. Is garlic harmful?"

"It smells terrible and makes my eyes water, but it won't kill me."

"What about crucifixes?"

"It's the same as any other holy object," Ben said. "If the wearer believes in the power behind it, the crucifix is effective."

"And you have to be invited into homes," Elora said. It seemed the rules of etiquette only grew stronger after undeath.

"Only those with living inhabitants who are fond of the building." He took another cautious sip of wine before pushing his cup away. "Aside from the threats posed by stakes, silver, and sunlight, vampires are quite inde-structible."

There was one more detail Elora wanted to know, something he'd hinted about earlier. "How were you turned after you left Madame Tremblay's that night"

It was like watching a factory shut down after a day's work. His expression shuttered and his lips formed a thin line. Elora felt like she'd crossed one. "I'm sorry."

He looked like he wanted to speak, but thought better of it. "Don't be. It's a tender subject for me. I'm not angry that you asked."

Relief filled her. She hadn't pushed away the closest thing she had to a friend at the moment. "I understand." She pointed to his mostly full teacup. "Are you going to finish that?"

He shook his head, and wordlessly, pushed the saucer to her.

CHAPTER 7

*B*en disliked the coal cellar.

He appreciated that Elora found him a private, light-proof hideaway, but he missed the comfort of a real bed. He stood up, dusted old coal dust from his trousers, and smoothed a hand through his hair. Perhaps it hadn't been the bed itself, which was old and smelled a little musty, he recalled, but the familiar, human comfort of sleeping on a proper mattress with blankets that made the bed so appealing. He'd done precious little of it since he was turned, instead sleeping in sheds or crypts, far away from prying and easily shocked human eyes. He thought about Elora and how she might look as she slept. In his bed.

With me.

He shook his head a little as if to clear the image itself from his mind. He washed up with soap and water from a bowl and ewer Elora dug out of a closet for his use. The notion stubbornly refused to fade away, sending a wave of sadness and longing cascading through him. He hadn't realized just how much he missed physical contact until she broke into Thorn House.

Uncharacteristic nervousness had his stomach in knots as he left the cellar to find Elora. It was just after sundown, and she would be awake yet for a few hours still. They were falling into a routine in the days since she was left stranded in Wand's Hollow, and Ben enjoyed having her around. It would be painful when train service finally resumed and she left Wand's Hollow, and him, forever.

That idea shouldn't feel like a wallop to the belly, but it does.

What reason could a human woman have to keep a lonely vampire company, anyway? Especially one as lively as Elora? He found her stretched out on a chaise longue in a parlor, stockinged feet up and crossed at the ankles, a book in her hands. Her boots rested on the dusty floor, one on its side, and her blouse's unfastened top buttons revealed the creamy column of her throat. The sight of it reminded Ben that he'd only had a tiny taste of her, of how much he wanted to again. He tamped down those urges. "Good evening."

She looked up and set the book aside, then sat, swinging her legs over the side of the chaise longue. "To you, too." She pulled a tarnished men's watch with a familiar fleur-de-lis pattern on its lid from her pocket and checked the time. "Eleven minutes after sundown," she reported. "You like to lay about in bed, don't you?" She snapped its cover shut, but before she could put it in her pocket.

Ben held out his hand. "May I?"

Elora looked at him quizzically but passed the watch over to him.

Ben held its steady weight in its palm for a moment, examining the piece. Just as he suspected, it bore the Lang Timepieces logo, engraved on the watch's underside in a looping scrawl, an unusual feature. His great-grandfather designed it and specially commissioned the dies used to mark each piece. The silver was tarnished, but he could see some care had gone into making it shine. Elora just didn't have the supplies to keep it perfectly clean.

The silver is tarnished.

The silver, *you utter bellend!*

As soon as he realized what he was holding, Ben dropped it.

Elora yelped and reached for it, nearly rolling off the chaise longue in the process. "Damn," she muttered. She clutched the watch tightly in her hand, but instead of lifting its lid to check the face for damage, she looked at Ben. "Are you all right? I completely forgot it's silver."

"I'll be fine." Pain flowed through his palm, radiating up his arm. He kept his hand clenched closed, to hide the angry red burn. He didn't want to worry her. "I should have considered that as well. My family makes those watches, after all."

Elora hauled herself up back to the chaise and he held out his unburned hand to steady her. She was warmer than he expected her to be. Had humans always been this warm? Had *he* ever been this warm? He reluctantly let her go.

"Your family makes Lang Timepieces," she said, incredulity in her voice.

He nodded. "I told you my father's family makes watches."

"My God." She shoved the watch in her skirt pocket and sat down on the chaise. "I didn't make the connection. I haven't heard a word about your disappearance." Her gaze fixed on his. "You did disappear, didn't you? You're not paying visits to your family and lying to them about being a vampire?"

He shook his head. "I wrote to them months ago. I'd taken an extended holiday to the Continent and haven't been in touch since. I was going to anonymously send them word that I'd died from something ridiculous in a few months' time."

"What kind of ridiculous?"

"Something that wouldn't be investigated and typical of a way a wastrel like I was would die. Drinking myself to death in a Parisian brothel was my first idea. Falling from a dirigible in a drunken stupor was another. I'm leaning toward the death by dirigible angle, myself, since I've already done it. I was thinking of a remote place, like the Swiss Alps, or over a river. It would be too difficult to investigate."

Something like sorrow crossed her face as she considered his answer. "That's terrible."

"Why?"

"That no one in your family has come looking for you. That they assume you would fall off a dirigible and wouldn't bat an eye."

It was sweet of her to think of his family, and himself in life, with that level of compassion, misplaced as it was. "Elora," he said gently, and took a seat next to her. She moved aside to give him more room, but it was still a snug fit. "I thought you understood that I wasn't a... very responsible person when I was alive. I was a rather selfish bastard, if you haven't picked on that by now. I'm more like your brother than you."

"What makes you think I'm not a selfish bastard, either?" she asked, arching an eyebrow. "You're forgetting that I came here with the express purpose of robbing my brother blind."

"You can't be a bastard," he pointed out. "I presumed

from everything that you've told me that your birth was legitimate."

"You're the descendant of the founder of Lang Time-pieces," Elora retorted. "One of the most powerful families in industry. I refuse to believe your ancestors would recognize an illegitimate child in their midst."

"And you would be correct. I'm being figurative. My point is I wasn't a good person."

"Because no one had any expectations of you and you did as you pleased?" She shifted just enough to face him, her knee touching his. He thought he could feel her body heat burning through their layers of clothes, and the sensation took his mind off the throbbing pain in his hand. "I'm sure you weren't a saint, but would you throw out your siblings as soon as you legally could, without even trying to help your sister find a husband first because you didn't want to be encumbered in any way?"

"I never had a sister, so…"

"But would you?"

His response was immediate. "No, of course not."

"Did you start vicious fights with others over trivial reasons, like someone not looking at you with the deference you thought you deserved? Or because you mistook someone for another, who you thought owed you money? Because Peter did all those things. He tossed a man into the Thames and was lucky the fellow didn't drown."

Ben was appalled. "None of those things. I was a lover, not a brawler. A drunken one, but peaceful."

"Then you aren't nearly the wastrel you think you were. A little irresponsible, certainly. Selfish, yes, and possibly a little stupid if you could fall off a dirigible but you weren't cruel for the sake of cruelty."

Everything she said was correct. "Being stupid and

selfish is how I ended up being turned and the lack of cruelty explains why I'm not a very good vampire."

"You don't have to tell me more about being turned," she said quickly. "I know that's a sore spot with you, just as Peter is with me. You can't be *that* bad of a vampire. You go out of your way not to eat people."

The pain in his hand reminded him of that. If he'd been feeding off humans as he was meant to, the burn would have healed already. It was vitally important that she continue to trust him, to want to keep being his friend, so he didn't mention that it was still bothering him. He'd figure out how to fix it later. "That's precisely why I'm a terrible vampire. We're supposed to be fearless beings, confident in the knowledge that we're superior to humans, and I don't think I am."

"You didn't harbor a superiority complex when you were human, which is commendable, sort of, considering your station in life."

"I didn't consider myself superior, but I didn't really notice others besides myself and my acquaintances. I noticed them after I was turned."

"Because sometimes you had to feed from them," Elora said.

"Yes."

"But you didn't kill them."

"No. I glamoured them and they forgot," he replied. "I still feel guilty about that. At first, my creator introduced me to humans who wanted me to feed from them. They were vampire's pets and they knew what they were getting into. The people who were just trying to stumble home from a tavern in the wee hours of the morning didn't. I couldn't keep doing that to people, no matter how much they might enjoy it in the moment after they stopped being terrified or if I glamoured them afterward." He was hungry for human blood, had been for weeks but he was not going to feed from someone who didn't want to be a meal. Never again. Just because he could do it with no consequences didn't mean he should.

"You told me before that they enjoy it."

There was a slight huskiness to her voice and a curious undertone. "Some people do," he said carefully. "Some vampires keep willing humans, too."

"You said you knew of a couple who were mates," she said. "Is that like married to vampires?"

"I don't know enough about the culture to know that but I'm sure they considered themselves married. It was unusual, to say the least. I don't think their relationship is one of an owner to a pet."

"What happens to pets?"

Anything could befall vampire pets. They weren't equal to the vampires who fed from them. He didn't want to lie to her. It was incredibly important that she trust him. "I think some are drained dry," he said. She stiffened a little next to him, and he hated his words made her feel that way. "Some are turned. Others have their memories wiped clean and are turned out into the streets to fend for themselves. It's not a good way to live."

"And you don't condone any of that."

It wasn't a question, it was a statement, and Ben suspected, a test. "No."

"And feeding from a human doesn't hurt," she said. Again, it wasn't a question.

"Not if it's done correctly."

"Did anyone ever feed from you when you were human?"

Just the once. While it started out pleasurably, it quickly turned into an agonizing, terrifying situation that led to him waking up in a dank Wapping cellar with his creator sitting in a corner smirking at him. "Yes." She didn't ask him any more questions about his turning, and he wasn't sure how he felt about that. He hadn't spoken of it to anyone. If other vampires knew how he'd cried and begged for his life at the time, they would've staked him themselves out of general principles.

"It wasn't bad," she said abruptly. "When you fed from me."

He hadn't really fed from her, as much as he wanted to. The memory of licking her fingertip clean overloaded his senses and flooded his body with a familiar heat for the second time in as many days. Still, he kept his voice neutral. "Oh?"

Her next words seemed deliberate, carefully chosen. "It was the opposite of bad. I suppose that makes it good. Is that what it was supposed to be like?"

Ben could hardly believe he was having this conversation. "I think so."

"So, it wasn't me being off," she said thoughtfully.

"Off about what?"

She shook her head. "It was just something I was thinking about. I…"

The sounds of chimes, discordant and screeching, filled the house. Ben jumped to his feet, and Elora screamed.

"What the hell was that?" Ben asked. His fangs fought to break free of his gums, undoubtedly some innate vampire defense coming to the fore.

Elora rose and pinched the bridge of her nose between her fingers. "The doorbell. Someone's here." She stepped into her boots and quickly buttoned them up. "I haven't heard that in years."

"That caterwauling is a *doorbell*?"

She hurried out of the parlor, a hurricane lamp in

hand. Ben followed. "Well, I'm sure it hasn't been maintained in years."

He realized, stupidly too late, where she was headed. "You're not seriously going to open the door?"

She didn't stop walking. "Do you have a better solution?"

"Yes! Ignore it!"

"And let someone break in, thinking the house is unoccupied? No," she said. She finally stopped, and holding up the lamp, glared at him. Her expression quickly shifted. "I can see your fangs."

"They tend to make an appearance when I feel threatened."

"Can you hide them?"

Ben tried to arrange his mouth around his fangs, and given how Elora's lips quirked upward at the attempt, guessed he had failed. "Sometimes."

"Then you can hide, and I'll deal with this." She resumed her walk.

"No!" he said and grabbed her arm. Too late, he realized he did so with his burned hand, and he couldn't keep himself from wincing at the pain.

"What's wrong?" she asked.

Any answer he might have received was cut off by another ear-splitting grind of rusting chimes banging together. "Nothing," he lied.

She shook him off and noticed his hand in the process. "What's this? Did my watch burn you? Why didn't you say anything?"

"It isn't important."

"Yes, it is!" She sighed in exasperation. "Look, stay nearby in the foyer, but I'm answering the door. If it's a neighbor, I have to make sure they'll leave us alone."

Ben liked how she said "us."

The hurricane lamp's light bounced along the walls, highlighting the occasional ugly oil painting until they reached the front door. "We're not finished talking about this," Elora said, with a pointed look at Ben's crotch.

He quickly realized she was actually looking at his hand, now hanging at his side with his fingers curled into his palm.

God, I'm an idiot. A lonely idiot.

Taking a deep breath as if to steel herself, Elora unbolted the front door and swung it open.

～

I MUST HAVE LOST my mind.

Would a vampire hell-bent on taking Elora for himself knock on the door? Especially when he could just waltz in, according to Ben, since she didn't own Thorn House? Logic dictated that it wouldn't be a vampire at her door, and logic was correct. Sergeant Sloan stood on the crumbling doorstep. Behind him, Elora could see his ornithopter, its basket empty.

"Good evening," she said in surprise. Her hurricane lamp quivered a little in her hand. It was getting heavy to hold up this high. "This is unexpected."

She didn't invite him in. He was human, but she still didn't trust him.

"Miss Stone," the sergeant said, inclining his head. He doffed his hat and held it under his arm. "How are you?"

"Very well."

"I'm here to tell you that train service will resume tomorrow afternoon. I thought you would appreciate hearing the news directly."

She didn't. For some strange reason, she was compelled to stay here, if only for another few days. *As if you don't know? You're here because you're fascinated with the vampire who looks at you like you're a slice of cake.* She tried to tell herself that her reaction to him was nothing more than a long-suppressed libido screaming to be finally free, but she knew she would be lying to herself. She wasn't ready to leave Ben to his own devices yet.

Sloan was waiting for an answer. She pasted a smile on her face and said, "Thank you for telling me, Sergeant." The part of her that guarded every memory of her mother reared its head, reminding her in her mother's voice that manners dictated the sergeant be invited inside for a cup of tea before he left, but Elora ignored it.

Sergeant Sloan didn't seem to be affronted at the lack of invitation. Instead, he looked over Elora's shoulder. "Hello, there."

Her stomach turned over, and she glanced behind her. Standing a couple of feet away from her, his pale face highlighted by the light of her hurricane lamp, stood Ben. She could tell by the set of his mouth that he was desperately trying to keep his fangs hidden.

"Oh," she said, hoping Sloan didn't notice the warble in her voice. "Sergeant Sloan, this is my friend, Ben. Ben, this is Sergeant…"

"Merritt Sloan." The sergeant stepped aside and held out his hand across the threshold.

"The sergeant's investigating the murder I told you about. To Sloan, she said, "You didn't say whether you caught him, though."

"It's an ongoing investigation," Sloan replied. "We have suspects, although none of them are from Wand's Hollow."

He didn't lower his hand or look at Elora, keeping his gaze pinned on Ben. Ben shot a frantic glance at Elora, and she hoped he wasn't about to do something stupid.

Ben stepped forward and held out his hand, letting Sloan shake it. "Sergeant," Ben said in deference. Trying to keep his fangs concealed gave him a bit of a lisp, which would have been funny had the situation not been so serious.

"Do you plan on returning to London in this case, Miss Stone?" the sergeant asked once Ben stepped away.

"In due time."

"Excellent." Sloan put his hat on his head. "I'm sure I don't have to remind you to keep your doors and windows locked. I don't expect the murderer is still in the area, but one can never be too careful."

"Of course. That's simply common sense."

"I'll leave you to it, then, Miss Stone, Ben… I apologize, I didn't get your surname."

"Lang," Ben said from directly behind Elora. His breath tickled her ear, an alluring sensation she'd missed since he last did it in the chapel, but she was too wound up to enjoy it.

"Mr. Lang," Sloan repeated. "Have a good evening." He turned away and walked to his waiting ornithopter.

Elora started to close the door, but couldn't help but watch, fascinated.

He hopped over the side of the basket, an unexpected and ungentlemanly gesture that was still oddly graceful. A gentle whirring filled the night air, and its wings raised themselves from the basket's sides. A moment later it lifted into the air and took off, clipping an overgrown tree's branches as it left the property before sailing away.

"Huh," she said. "I wonder what it's like to fly in one."

"They're cold and ruin your hairstyle," Ben said from behind her.

She forgot about the ornithopter and closed the door, bolting it behind her. "Why the hell did he show up?" she said. Noting that Ben's dental dilemma still hadn't resolved itself. "And why the hell are your fangs out?"

"That happens when I'm feeling defensive. I told you about that already."

"Can't you control them?" She knew she was being petty, but she couldn't help herself in that moment. Frustration welled up in her at the knowledge a police sergeant was keeping tabs on her. A horrifying possibility gripped her. "Perhaps he thinks I did it," she whispered.

"Do you mean the murder? Of course, he doesn't think you did it. I'm sure he's more curious about your reasons for wandering around a broken-down country home in the middle of nowhere, and why I'm here with you when we aren't married."

"Damn it." She leaned against the door and felt like an idiot. "I should've introduced you as my cousin. Now, he'll probably come back. I'm a fool."

"No, you aren't." His voice was soft and velvety. She didn't need to be enthralled to find it reassuring. "You're in a unique position, made complicated by a vampire who killed a human when you happened to be in the vicinity." He put a hand on her shoulder in what she supposed was a gesture of comfort, but it had a different effect. Her skin prickled, and she hated that her blouse was between their skin. Before she could further ponder that feeling, Ben hissed in pain and pulled his hand away. "What is it?" she asked. "Is your hand still bothering you?"

"Nothing." He folded his hand into a fist and kept it at his side.

"Ben, let me see."

They glared at each other for a few seconds, the hurricane lamp's light bouncing off his features. Finally, he sighed and held out his hand, palm up, to reveal an alarming red burn.

"Oh, my God," Elora said, reaching for his hand.

"I didn't want to worry you."

She had the distinct impression that he was about to say something she wouldn't like.

"Vampires heal faster when they're sufficiently nourished, much like humans."

"You need human blood," Elora translated.

"Yes."

"A fox won't help you with this?"

He shook his head. "No, but it's fine. It'll just take longer to heal, that's all. I can wait."

A strange combination of fear and excitement unfurled in her, and the rational part of her brain told her that she was crazy and shouldn't suggest what she was about to. But he was injured and in pain, and would need more than a bandage to heal him.

"You need to keep your strength up. For the sake of both of us." She squared her shoulders. "You can feed from me, if it'll help you."

Ben made a weird half-strangled sound. "What?"

"You were burned on my account."

"No, I wasn't. I burned myself for the stupidest possible reason. My family's factory manufactures those watches and I've known my entire life they were made of silver. If vampires were children in a schoolyard and they saw me do that, I would never hear the end of it."

"But you aren't schoolchildren and you're hurt," Elora said. "If you want some willing human blood, now's the time to take it, before I change my mind."

Lies. She had every intention of going through with letting him feed from her. She was too intrigued by the notion to refuse him. She held up the hurricane lamp to better see his expression and felt her eyes widen. His fangs were still extended, his pupils dilated until his irises were nearly black. More than that was the hunger on his face, and she was reminded of the night they met. He'd told her she smelled like lemon tarts. Here she was, the baker and the treat in one, offering herself to him. "Don't kill me," Elora added hastily. "You said you knew when to stop, and I trust you that you do."

Ben nodded. "I wouldn't dream of it."

"And don't turn me into a vampire. I don't want to rub it in, but I enjoy the feel of sunlight on my face."

"I did, too, when I didn't have to sleep off the previous night's outing."

"All right, then. Where's the best place to do this?"

His hungry look was replaced by one of confusion as he considered her question. "I don't suppose there's a best place. Wherever you feel most comfortable."

"Supper's choice?" she quipped as she began the walk back to the parlor. The chaise longue there seemed like a good spot. It could double as a fainting couch. Elora had never fainted until the night before, and being snacked on by a vampire seemed like the sort of event that would inspire unconsciousness.

Ben quickly caught up to her. "I've never asked anyone before."

"I know, you just enthralled them and erased their memories. Don't do that with me," she warned him. "I will find out, and I'll be very upset."

"How could you find out?"

"You'd let me know eventually," she said. "Whether by accident or design. You've told me almost everything else I've asked you. Why would that be any different?"

"I won't glamour or enthrall you and all of this is different, because I've never fed from a friend before. I want to get this right."

They had reached the parlor, and Elora set the hurricane lamp on a table. Its yellow light cast the room in shadows. The paintings on the walls depicted bowls of fruit and vases of wilting flowers, all of which looked a little ominous in the lamp's flickering light. Ben and his fangs didn't look ominous. Now that the shock of her offering herself to him had worn off, he looked... happy. Excited that he was going to do something he'd looked forward to for a very long time.

It was the same for her, she realized. She hadn't been held by anyone in years, let alone a man she was fascinated with. She sat down on the chaise and reached for her blouse's collar. Then she realized with mortification that she'd answered the door with the top buttons already unfastened. What on earth had Sergeant Sloan thought of that?

No, don't think of him now.

Deliberately, she unfastened another couple of buttons. "Vampires traditionally feed from the neck, don't they?" she asked, damning the quiver in her voice. She was intrigued, but now that she was partially undressing in front of a vampire, a wave of nervousness hit her.

"There are other places, but that's the easiest for now," Ben said. There was a husky quality to his voice that hadn't been there before. He took a seat next to her, their thighs touching.

Elora nodded, and pushed the fabric off her shoulder. She leaned her head to the side, exposing the side of her neck. "Do it."

Ben surprised her. Instead of sinking his teeth into her like an animal, he lifted a few errant strands of curly hair away from her neck and traced his finger along the spot where her pulse beat a rapid tattoo.

She closed her eyes. The sensation was cold but so welcome, making her breath catch in her throat.

He lowered his face, lips brushing against her skin, then the light scrape of his teeth. His fangs, she remembered. He had *fangs*. His bite was lightning fast and nearly painless. All Elora could focus on was an unexpected rush of pleasure that flooded through her, how hot her body felt under her layers of clothing, and Ben's weight against her. A moan escaped her, and she would have clapped her hand over her mouth if she'd had the strength.

Ben's arm snaked around her waist, pulling her closer to him, and she fell against the chaise's elevated end, taking him with her. His mouth sealed itself to her skin, the motion setting off fireworks through her body, and he mumbled something unintelligible against her. Her hands threaded through his hair, not wanting to let go of him but she did, hands moving down the back of his head to his shoulders, trying to pull him even closer against her. Her hands scrabbled at his shirt's fabric, when he pulled away.

He raised his head, revealing blood-stained lips, and stood up. The sight was unnerving and she touched the spot on her neck where he'd fed from. She felt tiny wounds there, but they felt like they were already healing.

"Thank you," Ben said, voice gruff. He held out his hand, now healed.

"Was that... was that it?" she asked. She couldn't help but feel disappointed, and she hadn't meant to enjoy it as much as she had.

He nodded. "I've had enough. Thank you."

"You're welcome."

He didn't meet her eyes, but he held out a hand to help her up. "You should get some rest. I'll watch over the house."

"Will you still be awake when I get up?"

"I'll go to the cellar before dawn," Ben said, not directly answering her question. "It's safest that way."

That irrational part of her brain urged her to invite him back to the bedroom she'd taken from him in the first place, but she tamped it down. He was acting oddly, and she guessed from the way he was dismissing her that he needed to be alone for a while.

I wish he would talk to me.

More than talk. Now she was curious how he would kiss her.

She merely nodded. "Good night, Ben."

CHAPTER 8

$\mathcal{B}$en stood outside Elora's closed bedroom door. He didn't have to press his ear to the wood to know she was sleeping deeply, to listen to the sounds of her steady breathing. If he focused on it long enough, he thought he might be able to hear her heart beating, her blood flowing through her veins.

Her blood.

He touched his lips, remembering the taste of her there. He felt like a new man, like he had finally managed to have a decent night's rest and a proper meal. He supposed in a way he had. And it was the best meal he'd ever eaten.

Elora Stone was a delicacy.

The sudden rush of lust had taken both of them by surprise when he bit her. He had experienced something similar with other humans, had been told that it was normal by other vampires, but it was entirely different with Elora. He'd been nearly overcome with the desire to kiss her and pull away the rest of her blouse to bare her to him, to feel her skin to skin. Her rapid intake of breath, the way she pressed herself against him and that moan told him she felt much the same way. He hadn't wanted to stop feeding when he did, but he had to. If he continued, he would have gorged himself, possibly hurting Elora. It was the last thing he wanted to do.

She was safe right now, under his watch, and he was determined to keep it that way.

He returned to Thorn House's main floor, to the parlor he was beginning to think of as Elora's. He tidied it a little, dusting off the furniture, wondering if she would notice. *Just over a year ago, I never would have cleaned a thing.* He hadn't had to. His family employed an army of servants so he never had to lift a finger, and he'd hired his own when he moved into his own rooms. He was still able to run his clean handkerchief over the shelves of dusty novels while he longingly thought of the woman upstairs, someone he could never have.

When his handkerchief was sufficiently filthy, he shoved it in his pocket and left the parlor for the house's front door, to see if the irritating sergeant saw fit to hover about the property. Once outside, he couldn't smell any humans, just the scent of the earth re-awakening after a long winter.

Sergeant Sloan shook my hand.

He would have immediately noticed how preternaturally cold Ben was. The notion was enough to strike a chord of fear into him, if he thought the policeman might have believed in vampires. As if one of his fellow creatures could read his thoughts, a dark shape flew from the untended trees and landed nimbly on his feet, a couple of yards away from Ben.

Some guard to Elora I've been, letting my vigilance down so much I didn't even sense another vampire in the vicinity.

Ben swallowed, any bravado he might have held gone as he stared down at Louis, a vampire compatriot of the one who turned Ben. Angelique, his creator, might be truly dead now, but Louis still stalked city streets and terrorized their citizens.

Louis didn't look like he'd arrived at Thorn House to stake Ben. Instead, he looked thoughtful, and in a low voice said, "So, this is where you've taken up residence."

The vampire had an accent Ben couldn't place, something vaguely European. Based on some of the events he mentioned experiencing in casual conversation, Ben suspected his original country no longer existed. "For the time being."

"We're very upset with Denis."

Forcing himself to keep his voice as steady as possible, Ben asked, "There's been a murder here. Was he the one who killed the village postmaster?" Was Louis here on account of Denis's disappearance, or Angelique's? Ben refused to believe it was strictly a social call.

"I don't know what the human did, but he killed the human here, yes. That deed has drawn a great deal of unwanted attention to this hovel." He managed to inject enough vitriol into the last word that Ben thought he could taste it. "Such an undignified and brutal way to enjoy one's food. But then, Denis was always undignified and brutal."

Ben nodded.

"Where is Denis?"

Ben sidestepped the question. "How did you know I was here?"

Louis raised a blond eyebrow. "I have my ways."

"It would be doing me a great service if you told me what those ways are," Ben said. "Seeing as I'm new to being a vampire, in the grand scheme of time."

Louis shrugged and inspected his sleeve. Under the

light provided by the moon and his own enhanced vision, he picked at a piece of lint. "I wasn't looking for you specifically. I was looking for Denis, as he's a friend of mine and prone to impulsive actions, like killing that human. Your being here is nothing but a coincidence." He looked up, suspicion reflected in his pale blue eyes. "And it's quite the coincidence. So, I will ask you again, where is Denis?"

"You weren't looking for me at all?"

"Why are you worried about that? Did you do something you shouldn't?"

Ben's mind flashed back to biting into Elora's neck, the reactions that kickstarted themselves in his body, how he'd had to push her away but Louis wasn't talking about Elora.

Does he know I killed Angelique?

It had been in self-defense, but Ben doubted that excuse would hold water in a court of vampires. She was a sadist, probably putting Denis to shame, but that was how London's vampires liked themselves to be. "No," Ben replied. "I haven't."

"Have you seen Denis? I enthralled a couple of this pissant town's humans to see what they remembered. He fed from them, but of course, he erased their memories. I could smell him all over that train station. I know he's been on this property. So." Louis's eyes narrowed and his lips thinned. "I'll ask you again. Where is Denis?"

"I don't know."

"I don't believe you."

Why was Louis arguing with him? Did he know Denis's desiccated, dusty remains were scattered around Thorn House's property? Or was he simply smelling the dust? It was so much easier to be rid of a vampire in the city. All Ben had to do to get rid of Angelique was dump her staked body in the Thames, where it would disintegrate in a matter of hours.

"It isn't like Denis to simply disappear. He's been here."

"He isn't here now," Ben said. "No one is. Now, are you going to argue with me until the sun comes up, or are you going to leave me be? There isn't a rule in vampire society that says we aren't allowed to leave London to be alone for a spell."

"There's a rule about not killing fellow vampires, and you already broke it when you killed Angelique."

Ben stilled. If he'd had a functioning heart, it would have skipped a beat. "I don't know what you mean," he said, damning the slight stutter that crept into his voice.

"Come now. Of course, you do. It's the worst-kept secret in London. We'll allow you that kill, because Angelique was a troublesome bitch who would have exposed all of us at some point or tried to feed from the queen, something stupid like that. We're willing to look the other way in certain circumstances."

Relief flowed through Ben and his knees nearly gave way. He wasn't going to be staked for killing the vampire who turned him.

"But Denis isn't like Angelique," Louis continued. "His absence will be missed if he's fallen to harm."

"Denis and I aren't friends."

"Yet he came here. I wonder what drew him here." He tapped his chin, the motion exaggerated, the look on his face that of a man who knew something his conversant didn't. Looking over Ben's shoulder, Louis called, "Why don't you come out, darling, and join our *fête*?"

Ben sniffed the air, caught the scent of lemon verbena, and physically recoiled. He whirled around to see the open door, the house's foyer dark and empty. Elora was nearby, probably listening behind the door. "Oh, God," Ben muttered.

Louis raised an eyebrow at the mention of a deity but didn't comment on it. "She smells delightful," he said. He stepped a few inches closer to Ben and delicately sniffed around him. "And you've partaken of her. Would it be an imposition to ask to share?"

"Yes."

"I've come all this way. It would be polite to let me have a taste." Without waiting for another protest from Ben, the older vampire pushed him to the side and up the crumbling stairs to the door.

And was stymied by the doorway.

Hope soared in Ben. Elora's presence was baking itself into the house's walls, offering a measure of protection against creatures like Louis. Like Ben. He hoped she would still allow him in the house, but his priority was keeping her safe. If that meant he couldn't re-enter, he would have to live with that.

Louis whirled around. "Tell your pet to invite me in."

"I'm not his pet," Elora said from behind the door.

Louis ignored her. "Ben, tell her now."

"No."

"No?" Louis sounded incredulous. "Who do you think you are, that you can refuse me your human pet?"

"I'm not his pet!" Elora shouted the words this time.

"She isn't my pet," Ben affirmed.

"Are you telling me that a human who isn't a pet knows of our existence?"

Ben hadn't thought this through at all. His mind worked quickly, trying to figure out a way that would keep him from being staked by either of them. "I'm working on that," he said. He heard her gasp from the house, the safest place she could be. *So much for Elora not wanting to stake me.* She had probably bolted from the foyer to break a leg off another table. Hell, she would probably carve his name into it. He wished vampirism came with telepathy, just to tell her that he didn't mean it.

"Tell her to let me in," Louis demanded again.

There wasn't a response from Elora, which only offered credence to Ben's theory that she was searching for a makeshift stake somewhere else in the house. "I don't think I can," he said.

If the house had reacted to Elora's presence during her short time here, recognizing her as its human owner, did that mean Ben could re-enter? He was sure that even the night before, Louis would have been able to stroll right inside. There was only one way to find out.

Ben took the steps two at a time, pushed Louis aside, and tried to walk through the threshold. It was like hitting an invisible wall. Electricity surged through him, the sensation excruciating. He'd tried to enter a few places uninvited shortly after he was turned and was painfully rebuffed, but it was nothing like this. He could see the light of a flameless candle quivering on the floor through the open door, which meant Elora was nearby. "Elora," he called. "I—I can't come back in." He chanced a glance at Louis, who wore a smug expression on his pale face.

The older vampire reached for Ben and grabbed a fistful of his coat. "Where's Denis?" he snarled.

"I don't know!"

"You're lying."

"I'm not!" Ben wasn't sure he would be able to escape Louis' grasp, but his enhanced strength told him otherwise. Ben easily pulled away, then pushed at Louis, who tumbled backward down the stairs. He landed in an undignified heap on the cobblestone path.

Louis immediately sprung to his feet, shooting a few feet up in the air in an impressive display of his flight prowess. He remained suspended in mid-air for a moment before gracefully landing on the ground. "I'm tired of this," he said. "Do I have to burn down the house to find out where Denis is? Or shall I return another night with some of his concerned compatriots?"

"Burning down the house will solve nothing."

"Your pet might say otherwise."

Elora was going to be on the next train out of Wand's Hollow if Ben had anything to do with it. At this point, he would push her on to the Liverpool policeman's ornithopter himself if it meant she could get out and stay safe. "Just return another night," Ben said wearily. "Let her get some rest. This isn't the time."

"You can't mean to keep this human without her being your pet!"

"I'll enthrall her," Ben promised. "That's within my skill set." Another lie. Oh, Elora was going to kill him, if she even invited him back into the house.

Something in Ben's tone must have convinced Louis that he had nothing to do with Denis's disappearance. That, or he was finally tired of the conversation. "I will return," Louis said.

Ben had no doubt the vampire meant it. Before Ben could respond, Louis took off in a blur of dark clothing, flying away for parts unknown.

Ben released a shaky breath, conscious of the motion. He didn't know he could still do that. He turned around and walked up the steps. "Elora?" he called through the open door. "Elora, could you invite me in, please?"

An unexpected sound greeted him, and with it, something in him painfully twisted.

She was crying. Muffled weeping reached his ears, a sound of terror and sadness.

"Elora," he tried again, lowering his voice to a whisper. "I didn't mean any of it. I'm not going to make you my pet or glamour you, I promise."

"I don't believe you," Elora said between sobs.

He moved as close to the door as he could without shocking himself. "Elora," he said in a stage whisper. "I swear to you I'm not going to hurt you or let another vampire hurt you. In fact, the first thing you're going to do tomorrow is get on the first train out of Wand's Hollow and get back to London. I insist on it. From there, you're going to board the first dirigible or train or whatever machine that will take you out of London. Anywhere in the world but you have to leave."

Her sniffling ceased for a few seconds. "What about you?"

"Don't worry about me. I can take care of myself."

"Denis was going to kill both of us," she said. The memory of it prompted a fresh wave of tears.

Ben was sure he could smell their salt. "But Denis is gone."

"And his friend came looking for him," she said, voice rising. "And he's coming back with his friends. You don't stand a chance against them."

That statement hurt his pride almost as much as the house's invisible barrier hurt his body, but unfortunately, it was accurate. "I'll cross that bridge when I get to it and you don't have to invite me back in, but I would greatly appreciate it if you did. If you're not going to, just let me know now so I can find a place to go to ground when the sun rises."

The door opened a few inches further, and Elora's tear-stained face appeared around the side of it. "You're really not going to glamour me into forgetting you?"

"Never. I would never do anything to hurt you, I swear. I needed Louis to leave us alone. And I don't think I *can* glamour you into forgetting."

He desperately hoped Louis's flight had already taken him miles away, so he couldn't hear their conversation. Ben couldn't smell the older vampire, but he hadn't smelled him when he was hiding out in that tree, either, but that could have been due to his reliving his feeding from her.

"I must be insane," Elora muttered. Louder, she said, "All right. Come in."

Ben touched the doorway with his finger, and a spark sizzled through him for his efforts. "I think you have to do it more formally. Try saying something like, 'Ben, I invite you into my home.' Use my name."

A watery sigh escaped her. "Ben, I invite you into my home."

This time, he was able to walk into the house, and he quickly closed and bolted the door behind him. "At least this offers you a measure of protection."

She sniffled. "How did that happen?"

"I suppose the magic only takes a day or two to take hold. You had fond memories and an attachment to the old chapel. Perhaps that attachment has extended to the rest of the buildings. At least this means a vampire can't just stroll in without an invitation."

"Including you."

"Yes, including me." He ran a hand through his hair, an old nervous gesture. "I meant it when I said you have to leave in the morning. You have enough things to sell by now and the train service has resumed. You need to get out of Wand's Hollow. Louis and his friends will be back."

She wiped her eyes with her nightgown's sleeve. No, not a nightgown, the edge of her shawl. She wore nothing but a thin shift and her traveling shawl over it, either in a bid for modesty or warmth, he wasn't sure. It was a distracting sight he couldn't afford now.

"What about you?"

"I'll be fine."

"No, you won't. It would be a passel of vampires against you." She paused. "Is 'passel' the right word?"

"I'm not sure it's important right now, but I'm not the person I'm worried about. I'm already dead."

"No, you're not."

"You still have marks from my fangs on your neck," he said gently. That was also a source of distraction. He'd never expected to see someone wearing his handiwork and to feel an accompanying sense of pride and possession to go with it. For a second, he understood the allure of keeping a human pet. *Do* not *start thinking of her in that way. Don't even entertain the fantasy. It's all right to like seeing her wearing your bite mark, but that's it.* He liked Elora's assertiveness, her willingness to speak her mind. Pets didn't do that. "Living people don't feed on their fellow humans," he reminded her. He thought he could see a blush creep to her cheeks but he didn't comment on it.

"My point is, you'll be hurt," she said. "I think you should come with me."

"What?"

"I'm not finished yet. I think you should come with me, and I want you to tell me about this Angelique person. You said you killed her. What happened?"

"Is my telling you about Angelique dependent on my escaping Wand's Hollow with you?"

"Possibly. I also want to know the circumstances under which you would actually kill someone."

"It was self-defense."

She nodded and sighed. "I would presume so. I'm going to get some wine. I think we both deserve it after tonight. Then you're going to tell me what happened with Angelique."

He didn't want to talk about her, but he would with Elora if it meant building a little more trust between them. "All right."

Elora fetched the bottle of wine they'd shared only a couple of nights ago, and she surprised him when she carried it directly to her bedroom. The hurricane lamp filled the room with a warm glow, making the gloomy space seem a little homier. She surprised him again when she tossed her shawl on the end of the bed, then slid into it. She held the bedclothes open for him. "I'd like some company if you don't mind."

Surprise at the invitation had him frozen in place for a few seconds, but he quickly recovered. Ben slipped out of his coat and boots, then slipped between the bedsheets with her. He missed sleeping in a proper bed, let alone sharing it with someone else.

Elora took a healthy gulp of wine directly from the bottle before passing it to him.

Ben demurred with a slight shake of his hand.

"You had some the other night."

"I'm not sure how it would sit right now," he replied. "I got to properly feed tonight."

Now, he could see her cheeks flame in front of him. She touched the bite mark on her neck. "Oh?"

"I feel good," he said. "Physically, I mean. We usually can't digest human food, and I don't know how I would do with wine on a full stomach." He watched as she adjusted the blankets around herself. "Not five minutes ago, you were worried I was about to glamour you into being my pet. Now, you're inviting me into your bed. What happened?"

She took another drink before answering and made a face. "I think my uncle left the worst bottles here." She leaned over the edge of the bed and set the bottle on the floor before facing Ben. "I didn't want to believe it. Most of me hoped that you were just trying to get that vampire to leave, but there was a tiny part that thought you were telling him the truth."

"What made you change your mind?"

"You could have enthralled me when I first arrived. You could've drained me dry when you licked the blood off my finger or bitten me, but you didn't. You've had multiple opportunities to make me do whatever you want me to, and you haven't. And then, after you finally got rid of your friend—"

"He's not my friend. Never has been."

"After you got rid of your *acquaintance*," she amended, "You told me I have to leave as soon as possible. Those aren't the actions of a man who wants to keep me for horrible purposes."

"I'm not a man."

She gave him a look that he guessed was supposed to be withering, and he smiled. "You are," she insisted. "You're a man who can't be near sunlight." A shadow crossed her face, and he wondered what she was going to say next. "You have to come with me," she said.

"What?" She'd mentioned that before, but he thought she was rambling aloud, trying to sort out her thoughts and fears. He sat upright, and she did likewise. He tried not to notice how she looked in the lamplight, at her thin nightgown that hid almost nothing.

"You can't stay here. They're looking for Denis. Your acquaintance doesn't believe you didn't kill him. And technically, you didn't."

"It would be far worse for vampires to mete out their justice on you than me," Ben said. "I'll recover, eventually. You won't."

"Neither of us has to suffer at all. Both of us can be on that first train out of here tomorrow. There has to be a way for you to safely travel in the daytime."

"No. I'll find another way. You get out of Wand's Hollow tomorrow and I'll find you wherever you traveled to."

"Can you fly away like the other vampire?"

"Louis."

"Is that a yes or a no? I seem to recall you're telling me that you fell off the back of a dirigible."

His pride was a little injured at having to tell her he couldn't fly. "I've tried to teach myself. But I can't fly, not yet."

"Look, could you just tell me if you can travel at all during the day?" she asked, a wheedling note to her voice. "I don't feel right leaving you here. Could you wear your overcoat, perhaps gloves, a mask and hat?"

"I can't be near any sunlight. It would fry me faster than a rasher of bacon in a hot pan. I would need to be in something light-tight and locked. Like a coffin."

"What about a trunk?"

The very notion sounded dreadful, and yet… "I suppose that would work. I would be uncomfortable, but if there was one to be found that was large enough, I could try it."

"We'll have to find one," Elora said. She threw back the bedclothes and stood up, grabbing her shawl. "There are trunks in the old duchess's suite. Help me pick one out."

Ben followed her as she rushed out of the room with her hurricane lamp held aloft. "You should get some sleep," he said in protest.

"I can sleep later," she said as she glided through the corridor on bare feet. They passed a few doors before she picked on seemingly at random, and immediately sneezed at the cloud of dust that rained down on them from the jamb. "Take a look."

The lamplight revealed a room with faded blue floral wallpaper and a stripped tester bed, the only indications that this room was once a lady's bedchamber. It was otherwise full of furniture: multiple wardrobes, mismatched chairs, piles of curtains, and several steamer trunks, all of which looked intact.

"Uncle Frederick never married. This room has been unused for as long as I've been alive. He used it for storage. I think he intended to sell these things but just forgot about them." She dragged the largest of the trunks closer to the doorway. "What do you think?" she asked. "I think it belonged to my grandmother."

Ben lifted the lid. A cloud of dust wafted up, and Elora sneezed again. The trunk was full of yellowed linens, which he pulled out and tossed aside. "Oh, dear," he said, surveying the trunk. He would fit into it, but he would have to fold himself in and hug his knees to his chest. It would be desperately uncomfortable, but when he inspected the trunk, he saw it had wheels affixed to its bottom, and still felt sturdy despite its age. That would make it easier for Elora to drag around on her own. "It's perfect," he said, hoping he forced enough enthusiasm into his voice to make her happy.

"Will you be awake? I never thought to ask, but do

vampires sleep? Or do you just lie awake while avoiding the sun?"

"Both," he replied.

Something in his voice must have given away his unease and dread at being locked up in a trunk for a train trip, because Elora's expression softened. "I'll make this as bearable as I can for you. We won't take the mail coach. I'll book us a private compartment on the train and see if there isn't a way for you to get out of the box and stretch your legs."

He was touched that she had considered that, but he doubted it would be possible unless private compartments had radically changed in the time since he was turned. "That's kind of you to offer, but you don't have to spend all your money on a private compartment."

"I have enough to pay for a ticket," she protested.

"So do I. I still have perfectly legal tender from the night I died. Please use it."

She looked at him blankly. "But it's your money."

"You do understand that dead people have no use for currency?"

She exhaled noisily, then pinched the bridge of her nose in frustration, something she'd done before. Ben smiled. "You do understand that I don't consider you a dead man? Just one in an altered state of being?"

He did, and that knowledge would forever leave a part of him feeling warm and fuzzy. Loved, almost. For that alone, he was willing to endure a daytime train trip, locked in a steamer trunk that had to be half a century old. "Yes. I'll remember that, as long as you remember that I can afford to have us travel in style. Tomorrow morning, you're going to buy a first-class private compartment on the first train that will take us to London."

The relief on her face was palpable, and he could tell it wasn't just for herself.

There's that warm feeling again. Even when he was alive, he hadn't felt that. "You should get some sleep," Ben said. "I'll wake you up before dawn, so you can help pack me away."

She looked at the open trunk, then back at Ben, her lower lip worried between her teeth. "You would let me know if something went wrong in there, wouldn't you?"

"Of course."

That answer seemed to placate her. She picked up the hurricane lamp and carried it out of the room. "You still haven't told me about Angelique."

The last thing he wanted right now was to talk about Angelique. "Another night."

"You promised."

"You assumed," he said. "And assumed correctly. I'll tell you about her, but not now." It was an ugly story, and Elora had seen enough ugliness for an entire lifetime since they met.

She sighed. "Fine, I suppose I'll have to wait." Once in the bedroom, she slipped off her shawl again, wearing nothing but her nightgown, and Ben forced himself to look away. "Will you stay with me? I haven't adjusted any of your light proofing." She gestured at the heavy drapes, tied shut. The exterior shutters on the windows were pulled closed, too.

Ben had made sure of that his first night in Thorn House. He was flattered that she asked. "Of course."

"I sort of evicted you from here in the first place, didn't I?" She slid into bed and drew the bedcovers around her.

"That's all right. The cellar is a better choice for a vampire."

"But you like beds." She patted the spot next to her.

Ben gladly accepted her invitation, even though he knew he wouldn't be there all night. He would wait for her to drift off, then collect his scant belongings, and practice folding himself into unimaginable shapes to fit into a steamer trunk.

But until then, he was content to while away the night with Elora.

CHAPTER 9

hank God the largest steamer trunk in Thorn House had wheels. Whoever thought to add that feature was a genius.

The wheels provided less reassurance than Elora expected as she pulled the trunk behind her. She was gripped with terror that something would go wrong. That the old hinges would snap apart, the wheels falling off, someone trying to steal it. As it was, when she bought her train ticket from Wand's Hollow's murdered postmaster's son, all she could do was wait inside the station with the trunk at her feet, hands folded into each other to keep them from quivering.

The very last thing she wanted to do was look suspicious.

It was the warmest day Elora had experienced since spring took hold, and she hated it. Her clothing was too heavy in the stuffy station, but she didn't dare go outside for some fresh air and leave her precious cargo behind. Nor did she want to drag the trunk outside to wait for the train, for fear something would go wrong and Ben would fall into the sunshine, only to burn to a crisp in front of her. That was all from her imagination. She wasn't sure how sunlight worked on vampires, if its effects were gradual or immediate, and asking Ben about it felt rather crass.

We trust each other.

She couldn't believe she gambled on her life and won last night. She was correct about Ben's lying to Louis about her, about what happened to Denis. What would have happened if she had been able to sleep and hadn't gone looking for Ben for some company? Even though he pushed her away after he bit her? The memory of his bite made her feel flushed all over, and she instinctively reached for her throat. The marks left by Ben's fangs were hidden behind a scarf wound around her neck. It was too warm to wear it, but she didn't want to draw any curious looks or questions.

It was half-past noon when the London-bound train arrived, and Elora had never been so glad to see Wand's Hollow behind her when she boarded it. A porter helped her lift the trunk aboard the train, but she shooed off his attempts to haul it to her private compartment.

"It's a short distance, considering," the porter said when he opened the door to the compartment. "Quite the style to travel in when it's just a couple of hours."

Elora tried not to let her irritation and worry for Ben show. "Sometimes, it's nice to treat oneself," she said.

"Of course, madam," the porter replied without missing a beat. "Shall I bring you anything for your journey?"

Ben had plied Elora with all the notes he had on his person, far more than she ever needed for the ticket. Would he be cross if she spent some of it on herself? He said he had no use for it anymore. "A bottle of sherry and whatever sandwiches are available right now. Two of them." She would save the sherry for later. Perhaps Ben would want some.

"Right away," the porter replied.

Elora's mouth nearly watered at the thought of the sandwiches on the way. She'd eaten nothing but the thin soup she'd cooked over a fire since her second day in Wand's Hollow. She waited impatiently until the porter returned with a small bottle of sherry, a glass, and two roast beef sandwiches, her favorite. She locked the door behind the porter and closed the drape on the compartment's tiny window before tapping on the trunk. "Ben?" Her voice was a stage whisper.

A muffled thump greeted her in response.

"Do you want me to open the lid?"

She heard an indistinguishable stream of words, followed by another thump. Grinning, she unlatched the trunk's lid and lifted it a few inches, to peer at the piles of yellowed linen sheets inside. "Ben?" she said again. "I made it as dark as I could. Do you want some air?"

Ben struggled in the sheets for a few seconds before his pale fingers appeared and pulled the sheet away just enough to reveal his eyes. He blinked. The motion was almost owlish. "I'd nearly forgotten what afternoon feels like."

"Is it dark enough for you?"

He hesitated a fraction of a second too long.

"It isn't," Elora said, answering herself. She plucked her hat from her head and put it over his eyes. "How's that?"

"Well, it smells like you."

"I would expect it to."

"I mean, it smells good," he clarified. "You really do smell incredible."

"Is it because of..." She was loath to say it, to remind Ben of what Denis pointed out the night they met. It was simply too embarrassing to discuss such a thing with a vampire who had all but admitted to being an unrepentant libertine when he was alive.

Ben seemed to have picked up on what she was hesitant to talk about. "That's part of it," he said. "A very small part. You would still smell as good as you do no matter what."

The compliment warmed her in a way the spring heat didn't. She couldn't keep herself from repeating the quip he said to her shortly after they met. "Like a bakery."

Elora had never considered herself the giggly or swoony type, but she thought that might change now that she was hearing Ben's words. She couldn't help it. She received compliments so seldom, and he was still the most attractive man she'd ever met.

Part of her wanted to ask for more, but the rational side of her changed the subject. It was something she wanted to ask since the night before, but hadn't known how to bring it up, or if she should. *I suppose it's better late than never.* "I liked it when you fed from me."

From under her hat, Ben made a wordless, half-strangled noise.

"But you just pushed me away," she continued. "I thought I might have done something to put you off, or my blood didn't taste right."

"Oh, God."

"Is that 'oh, God' a 'damn it, she's figured out she tastes terrible' sort, or have I simply breached vampire food etiquette?"

"Neither," he replied. "You taste as good as you smell. As far as I know, you haven't made any etiquette missteps." He struggled with the linen for a moment, then lifted the hat just enough so Elora could see his face, and the earnestness reflected in his eyes. "I had to get away from you before I did something stupid."

A strange combination of fascination, hope, and fright filled her. Even though he was bent at odd angles as he traveled in an old trunk to save himself from the sun, she had to remind herself that she was dealing with a vampire. A man who survived off the blood of humans. She couldn't keep herself from asking, "Like what?"

"I think this is a conversation I would rather have when I can look you in the eye without worrying about cooking myself alive." He lifted the hat again. "You did nothing wrong, Elora. I promise."

Disappointment coursed through her. "Of course. It's good to know I didn't spoil everything."

"You didn't." Now it was his turn to change the subject. "Have you given thought to where we'll stay in London?"

Despite the doubt his words cast over her, Elora liked how he said "we." "I thought I would find us a room to let."

"I mean when we get there. Our immediate need for a room. Did you mean to leave me at the King's Cross left luggage while you looked for an available room in a boarding house?"

Now, she felt foolish. "I hadn't considered it."

"That's all right, this is novel to me, too. When the train arrives in London, find a steam cab, and go to The Savoy. You should have enough funds to pay for all of that."

"The Savoy?" Elora had never been. She scarcely had the opportunity to hire cabs, steam or otherwise, due to her perpetual lack of money. Her own feet were good enough for her.

"We'll stay there a night or two and then we'll decide where to go next."

"Do you mean to go with me wherever I decide to run away?"

He sat up so he could face her. "If you'll let me."

She had the impression that if she sent him on his way when they reached London, that he would leave her. It felt good to know he would listen to her, yet at the same time, she already hated the idea of being away from him. It wasn't just how he made her feel when he drank her blood or the way he looked at her like she was someone important. She had been so lonely for so long, and she'd found another lonely soul to be a companion to. She nodded, and he looked visibly relieved to see the motion.

The effect was spoiled when he yelped, "Fuck!" and snuggled back in the trunk with the sheets over his face.

"Are you all right?"

"It was hot," Ben said, his voice muffled. "But I don't think I'm burned."

Sunlight poked through the compartment drape's edges, leaving thin beams on the train floor. "Could you close the lid?" he asked. "I'm going to try to get some sleep."

Elora took her hat back from the pile of sheets. "I'll be right here if you need me," she said and closed the lid.

NEVER IN HIS life had Ben ever been more grateful to stretch.

He couldn't believe he made the entire journey from Wand's Hollow to The Savoy Hotel cramped in a trunk, during lethal daylight hours. Not only had he done so, he actually managed to catch a small amount of sleep. Any exhaustion evaporated when he looked at Elora, at how her blond curls escaped the severe knot on the back of her head. The room's electric lights gave them a halo effect. She looked like an angel, and in a way, she was.

She didn't have to bring him back to London, but she'd chosen to. He was determined not to mess that up for her.

He hated that she looked so aggrieved. "Was everything all right when you signed into the hotel?" he asked. Elora had pulled the room's drapes shut against the late afternoon's setting sun, but he avoided the windows all the same. The memory of the sun's warmth on his skin in the train was a harrowing one, even though it hadn't done any damage to him.

"I've never been here. I was looking forward to finally seeing the inside of this place, but it isn't my world. I don't belong here."

"Was anyone impolite to you?"

"Not at all," she replied. "On the contrary, they were very helpful. I took the staff by surprise when I appeared in all my dusty and wrinkled glory, bearing a huge trunk on wheels and asking for a room."

"You aren't wrinkled."

She gave him a look that questioned his intelligence and pointedly shook out her skirt which Ben now noticed was creased. "Oh," he said. "I see. I suppose my clothes are in the same condition. We're a matched set."

That drew a smile from her, and inspiration struck him. "Can you send for a porter?" he asked.

Elora looked around the room until she found the bell pull near the bed. "What for?"

"It's a surprise."

A porter promptly appeared, and Ben took him aside to make his request. Using a sheet of hotel stationery left on the cherrywood secretary, he wrote a list of his requirements before sending off the porter.

"Did you glamour him?" Elora asked when the door closed.

"Yes, but not in a bad way," Ben replied. Pride surged in him at the knowledge that he had finally enthralled a sober human with success. "He'll believe you placed the order I just made."

She eyed him suspiciously. "What do you have planned?"

"Nothing nefarious."

"That's exactly the kind of thing a person would say if he planned something nefarious."

He sighed. "Can't I do something nice for you?"

"Yes," she said, surprising him. "But you should know that I'm not used to people doing nice things for me."

She had alluded to as much in their conversations, and had been turned away from her family as soon as her brother could be rid of her. Ben thought back to his own upbringing, of the birthday parties his mother held for him, how his older brothers doted on him when he was small, and he felt nothing but sadness at their unequal treatment. "I'm taking you out," he announced. "As soon as it's safe for me to leave the hotel. We're going to have a night on the town. I asked the porter to bring back appropriate evening clothes for us."

"You didn't!" The smile that bloomed on her face told him she believed him, and that she was delighted with the idea.

"I did," he reiterated. "And since our lovely home for the night is equipped with it, why don't you take a nice soak in the bathtub?"

She raised an eyebrow. "Do I smell?"

"Always delectable." That remark made spots of color

flame high on her cheeks. "I thought you would enjoy it after days in a country house without any modern amenities and a train trip."

"I would and I should tell you I was just teasing. I know you like how I smell."

"Tease me all you like," he said, as she strode into the bathroom, closing the door behind her.

ELORA GAZED up at the night sky, the stars blotted out by the tall gaslights lining the street and flameless lamps perched in the merchant stalls of Covent Garden's night market. A hot air balloon as red as the evening dress she wore, slowly descended to a raised platform where a few people queued, waiting for a turn to sail into the air for a few moments.

"Do you want to take a ride?"

She had the vague impression from his tone that Ben had already asked her that question and she had been too spellbound to notice, thanks to the aerial trickery in front of her eyes. She finally tore her gaze from the hot air balloon away to look at Ben, who wore an expectant look on his face. "Are you serious?" He had already spent so much acquiring their evening clothes and supper for her in a private dining room at The Savoy that she couldn't wrap her head around more. As it was, she was overwhelmed with the sights she took in as they strolled through London at night, arm in arm. He cut quite the dashing figure in his new suit and matching hat, his dark hair having been trimmed by a hotel barber earlier that evening. Elora hadn't known hotels employed barbers until that moment.

"I want to see you looking like that again," Ben said,

and took her gloved elbow, steering her toward the queue for rides. "I like it when you smile."

"Do you have an ulterior motive?" she asked, letting him guide her in place.

"What motive could I possibly have?"

Elora tilted her head to the side where he'd bitten her. The mark had faded more quickly than she expected, but she was still grateful for the night that hid it.

His eyes widened, and something sparkled in them under the lights. "No ulterior motive. Is it so difficult to believe I simply want you to enjoy yourself?"

It was, Elora realized. She couldn't remember the last time she had done anything for fun except sitting in her drafty attic room in Mrs. Phillips's boarding house, reading penny serials when she could spare the coin to buy them. Taking a ride in a hot air balloon felt so over the top, so decadent, that she could hardly believe she was doing it.

He was waiting for an answer.

"Yes," she finally said.

"Well, that changes tonight." His hand reached around her back and squeezed her shoulder, a gesture of affection that halted the breath in her lungs for a half-second.

Neither of them spoke until it was their turn to buy their fares, which Ben did. He made a bit of a fuss helping Elora into the basket, his fingers clasping her gloved ones in a way that made her wish she wasn't wearing them, propriety be damned.

Her excitement about their flight was colored when the basket door closed behind them. "Is it just us?" she asked nervously.

"The balloons are tethered to the ground," Ben said. "They're using pulleys to control them. See?" He pointed at a group of men wearing matching gray uniforms, standing behind an enormous copper machine that looked like it was loaded with giant spools of thread. They pulled and pushed levers seemingly at random. The hot air balloons around them rose and lowered in the air.

Their balloon gave a little jump and Elora shrieked, grabbing on the basket's edge as it began a slow ascent. The sound of forced air filled her ears, and the balloon's speed picked up. "Oh, my God," she said, not daring to look over the side.

"Have you ever been aboard a dirigible before?" Ben asked gently.

"Never." She kept her eyes on the basket's floor, on Ben's shoes. Like her, he was wearing a new evening suit, the height of fashion. She supposed from the way he moved and walked in it that he was used to it, that he missed that part of his life. "I'm sorry," she said without looking up.

"What for? It's your first time in the air, and it's perfectly safe."

Elora's stomach felt like it had twisted itself in knots, but she ripped her gaze from the floor and forced herself to look over the basket's edge. She gasped. Covent Garden's night market appeared small and sparkly below the hot air balloon, the people moving about in their evening finery like tiny automatons. The rest of London was spread out before her, looking like a massive model, an expensive toy that parents wouldn't let their children play with. When she turned to either side of her, she saw matching red balloons either lifting or lowering, the figures inside them occasionally squealing with excitement.

Elora didn't want to waste this opportunity. She might never have a chance to experience flight ever again. She swallowed her lingering nausea and turned around in the basket, doing everything she could to take in as much of the city as she could before the balloon landed.

"Better?" Ben asked.

She nodded and smiled. "Better. Thank you."

"I meant it when I said I don't have any ulterior motives," he said quietly. "You don't have to feed me for me to be your friend."

When was the last time Elora had had a friend? Perhaps when she was still in the schoolroom, before she had to end her education after her parents died, or when she still attended church services. Certainly not since she'd been an adult. There was something he needed to know. "I like it when you feed from me."

He cleared his throat before forming a response.

Elora smiled. She did enjoy teasing him.

"But you don't have to," he reiterated. "I don't ever want you to think you're obligated to feed me."

The hot air balloon swayed a little, bobbing side to side, and Elora again held on to the basket for dear life. Sending a quick, nervous smile to Ben, she asked, "Have you seriously tried to fly?"

"I've made some unsuccessful attempts. I wouldn't jump out of the basket and not expect to have every bone in my body not broken when I landed."

"Is there anything I could do to help you?"

"Why? Do you want me to squire you away like a villain in a bad penny serial?"

"I *like* those bad penny serials and I…" She felt herself blush, but she forced her next words out, hoping she wasn't making a mistake. "I wouldn't—I wouldn't object to you 'squiring me off,' although I suppose it isn't squiring if I agree to it."

He didn't reply for what felt like an eternity.

Elora fought the urge to squirm in place, and a growing sense of panic told her she'd just made a terrible mistake in confessing her feelings.

Finally, he said, "You're very squirable."

Cautious hope flared in her. "I am?"

"Very."

His hand tilted up her chin, his fingers lingering over her jaw and tracing a line down her throat, over her rapidly beating pulse. Excitement thrummed in her like a drumbeat, steady and insistent, until his lips met hers, cool and firm.

It was her first kiss. She grabbed his shoulder, unable to tell if her unsteadiness was due to her new shoes, the hot air balloon, or Ben himself, or a combination of all three. The balloon swayed and his arms snaked around her waist to bring her closer to him. Pinpricks of pain interrupted the moment, and she involuntarily pulled away.

Ben immediately released her and raised a hand over his mouth.

Elora touched her lips, but couldn't see any traces of blood on her red silk gloves. Both of them knew what had just happened. "It's all right," she said. Summoning all her courage, she raised herself on tiptoe to kiss him again. Her aim was a little off, landing on the corner of his mouth, but he corrected that, lips and fangs crushing her mouth.

And Elora loved it.

His tongue flicked against her lips, demanding entrance, and she was happy to oblige. He clasped her hips against him, wedging her between his body and the basket. The hot air balloon jolted and sank a few feet. Elora started, breaking their kiss, and tried not to shriek.

Ben pressed his forehead against hers, his breath coming in short pants. "It's all right," he murmured. "The balloon's descending. We'll be back on the ground in a few minutes."

His tongue darted out and licked at the spots where his fangs pricked her, a motion so quick that Elora didn't have time to react to it. It sent a bolt of heat straight through her, as did his eyes when they met hers, lazy and half-lidded. He had been as affected by their kiss as she had been.

His fangs retracted by the time the balloon landed on its platform, and he took Elora's arm to lead her out of the basket. Nodding at the attraction's attendants, he guided her away from the hot air balloons.

Elora no longer cared about where they were going next. All that mattered was that they spent the precious amount of time they had together before dawn broke.

"Ben!" The unfamiliar voice calling for him had both of them turning around.

Elora's euphoria was replaced by a sense of terror. Had Louis or one of his friends tracked them down? There were too many humans here to conduct vampire business. Ben's face, already pale, was drained of color. "Shall we run?" Elora whispered to him.

A man approached them, an attractive and heavily pregnant woman at his side. He wore a fashionable set of evening clothes, not unlike Ben's, and when Elora looked at him closer, she saw he bore a striking resemblance to Ben.

"No," Ben replied. Louder, he said, "George?"

"Ben!" the man said. Both of them approached Elora and Ben, delighted smiles across their faces. "You absolute ingrate, you didn't tell us you were back in England," he added. Despite the use of the word "ingrate," he said the words with affection.

"I only just returned," Ben stammered. Before Elora could question him about it, he took a deep breath. "George, this is Miss Elora Stone. Elora, meet my brother and his wife, George and Josephine Lang."

CHAPTER 10

*B*en couldn't believe this was happening.

He smiled in a manner that he hoped was gamely and let George clap him on the back. His sister-in-law, Josephine nodded her head at him and beamed. *I can't believe I didn't think of the possibility of this occurring but then, when did George and Josephine ever go for a stroll through the Covent Garden night market?* "I've only just arrived back in London," Ben said. His mind working frantically, he said, "I hadn't planned to stay long."

"We were getting worried," George said. "We hadn't heard from you for months. Father was talking about hiring a private investigator to look for you in Europe. The last we heard, you were swanning about Italy."

That was what Ben told the family in his final letter to them. "I was and I fully intend to return to Europe shortly. With Elora," he added.

Elora gave him a quick look that questioned his intelligence before bobbing her head up and down.

"I didn't know you found a companion," Josephine said. "We're delighted to meet her."

Josephine, like the rest of the family, knew about Ben's reckless life as a libertine, and the last thing he wanted was for Elora to be considered as a mere companion. "She's my fiancée," he blurted out.

"What?" muttered Elora under her breath at the same time George and Josephine offered their congratulations. She pasted a smile on her face and graciously accepted them an eighth of a second later.

Josephine clasped Elora's hands in her own. "I can't tell you how happy I am to hear this news," she said. "Marriage does a man good. Lord knows Ben needs it."

"Oh, my God," Elora said. Her voice was pitched a little higher than normal, and Ben had no idea what that meant beyond her panic at the situation. She recovered quickly enough. "It's so nice to meet you, Mrs. Lang."

"Please, call me Josephine," she said. "We'll be sisters soon enough." She looked at the queue for the hot air balloons. "Did you just take a trip into the sky?"

"We did. It was my first time in a hot air balloon." She sent a look to Ben that nearly had his fangs out again, but he willed them away. At least she could keep her sense of humor during this trial.

"Oh, I've wanted to do that since this was set up. But the doctor thinks I should wait until after the baby arrives, and then we'll take the children with us. Ben, you're going to be an uncle again in a few weeks."

"My felicitations to both of you," Ben said. While George and Josephine doted on their three children, Ben learned early on in his life that while he liked children well enough, he didn't deal with them particularly well. His nieces didn't listen to him and one of them liked to bite others. *So am I, so I suppose I can't really judge them for that anymore.*

"How long are you back in London, then?" George asked.

"Just for a couple of days," Ben replied. "Then I'm taking Elora back to Italy."

Josephine and George's smiles faded. "But you haven't married yet," Josephine said in a stage whisper.

Oh, damn, he'd forgotten that his more traditional older brother would disapprove of Ben spiriting away a woman before he married her. "We'll elope," Ben promised.

"Mother and Father will be very upset if you do that," George said.

"I'm sure you see why I wanted to keep it a surprise." Desperation clawed at him as he thought about ways to extricate himself and Elora out of this mess. The only thing he could think of was using his glamour but could he erase the encounter from both of their minds at the same time, or without one noticing he was doing it to the other? He'd never attempted either thing before.

George's disapproval of his not marrying Elora aside, Ben desperately missed his older brother. He missed his whole family. He would dearly love to sit in his mother's fussy little parlor, her favorite place in the house, and introduce Elora to her.

For a few seconds, he let himself imagine he was human again, that he and Elora met by chance in, say, a bookshop. Ben couldn't remember the last time he frequented one and she had mentioned being too poor to buy books, but in his fantasy, both of them patronized bookshops. He would look up from a shelf of something boring and academic, perhaps astronomy. He would see sunlight streaming through the windows, catching Elora's dark blond curls peeping out from beneath her hat, and introduce himself …

None of that happened, or would ever happen.

"Ben?" said George curiously.

He snapped out of musing about what-ifs. "Why don't we visit Mother and Father tomorrow night?" Ben asked. Elora's hand tightened around his arm, and he felt the message there. She wanted to know what the hell he was thinking. *I'm thinking I miss my family and I never got to say goodbye to them before I died.*

"I'm certain they would love that," George replied. "Josephine and I will be there, too. So will the children. They've asked about you since you left, you know."

"Hm." If they'd cared at all, it would have only been because they didn't have anyone to bite but there was something else he had to consider. "We won't be able to stay for supper," he said. "Perhaps we could stop by afterward."

Both of them looked surprised. George said, "But Mother will be disappointed."

"I apologize for that," Ben said. "I really do, but we won't be able to stay."

George raised an eyebrow, and Ben had the feeling that he was going to be roped into sitting at his parents' supper table, his objections be damned. "It was lovely to see you," Ben said. "If you'll excuse us, Elora and I have to return to our rooms." He nearly said, 'The Savoy' but stopped himself in time. He didn't want his brother to know where he was staying, in case George got it in his head to stop by for a visit.

"You're staying together?" George said, disappointed. "Oh, Ben."

"When Mother meets Elora, she won't care," Ben retorted. "We're both adults."

"What do Elora's parents think of this arrangement?" Josephine asked.

"My parents have passed on," Elora replied. "Quite a number of years ago."

George and Josephine exchanged a glance, and Ben could read Josephine's mortification at having asked such a question. He used that as his opportunity to escape. "We'll visit Mother and Father tomorrow at seven," he said.

They said their goodbyes to each other, and Ben led Elora away from the night market to the street that still bustled with people at this late hour. "Why did you do that?" she hissed in his ear.

"Because they're my family," Ben said. "I miss them. I love them."

She stiffened next to him. "I'm sorry. I didn't mean to be rude. I just don't share those feelings about my family, and I forget that others are raised by people who love them."

Something in her voice tore at him, made him want to reassure her that he would never abandon her, but he doubted she would believe him. They hadn't known each other long, and ultimately, he was a predator and other predators were after him. The fantasy of meeting her in an ordinary way, of courting her in an appropriate fashion, wouldn't leave him. Ben had never been inclined to seek out a spouse, but if he had met Elora when he was alive, he might have changed that outlook.

"You do understand that your family's treatment of you wasn't your fault?" he asked.

"Yes, but that doesn't make it hurt any less."

It was the first time she had spoken of the pain her brother and uncle inflicted on her after they left her behind. This wasn't Elora out for revenge by stealing everything of value from a duke's dilapidated country house, or a flip remark brushing off something terrible that happened to her. It was her truth and experience, distilled to a few words.

"I can't make it stop hurting," Ben said. "But I can stay with you so you won't be lonely anymore." He wished they weren't in public, so he could kiss away that look of uncertainty and apprehension from her face. Kiss, and more.

But she relaxed. "Thank you."

"For not leaving you?"

"For that, and for being kind." She linked her gloved hand through his. "For everything you've done so far tonight."

"I should remind you that we're in this position because you hauled me across the country in a trunk. I will always be indebted to you."

"It was the right thing to do. You would've done the same for me. No, I had a lovely evening. I got to pretend to be someone for a night, I had a nice meal with good company, we toured the Covent Garden night market, and we took a ride up in a hot air balloon." She looked up at him knowingly. "And I had my first kiss, which was better than I could have expected."

"That was your first kiss?"

"Yes. I thought you knew. You know about the other… thing, I suppose." Her voice dropped to a whisper. "Me being a virgin. I thought you could tell like the other vam —the others." She'd caught herself in time. They were still in public, still surrounded by people.

"I actually don't care about what they do. I'm surprised no one's kissed you until now. You're eminently kissable."

"Don't you mean edible and kissable?"

"I mean both."

They approached the street, and Ben hailed an oncoming steam cab, to take them back to The Savoy, where he would show her just how eminently kissable she was.

⁓

NERVOUSNESS AND EXCITEMENT thrummed through Elora as she and Ben stepped into the lift. She didn't know what to expect, *if* she should even expect anything at all. She'd never had a physical connection with anyone before, and she would be damned if she would waste this opportunity with him.

They were quiet until they reached their room and Ben locked the door behind them.

A wave of shyness crested over her, and she started unfastening the row of buttons that marched along the length of her red silk gloves, starting with her left. "Thank you for arranging the clothes," she said, not looking up as she flicked open each tiny silk-covered button. "I can't remember the last time I wore anything like this."

"Red suits you." He was in front of her in a flash, working on the buttons more deftly than she could. "You should wear it more often."

She resisted the urge to laugh, knowing it would hurt his feelings after paying a compliment but she was still unsure how to accept it. She'd worn castoffs purchased from cheap secondhand shops for years. She doubted she'd ever seen anything red in that time.

"Thank you."

He made short work of the gloves and draped them off the arm of a stiff-backed chair.

"I don't know how to do this," she blurted.

Ben tilted his head to the side, waiting for her explanation.

Mortification burned hot in her, but she forged on. "I'm sorry."

"For what?"

"I don't know," she replied. "You know, I think I just spoiled everything now."

"You didn't. Although I'm not sure what you think you spoiled."

She felt like an idiot. "You kissed me on the hot air balloon."

Confusion crossed his face. "Did you not like it?"

"I did. A lot. But I don't know what I'm supposed to do next, now that we're here."

Understanding dawned in his eyes. "Oh, I see. You're expecting me to flip your skirt over your head and have my way with you."

"Well, not exactly. This dress has to go back to the place you rented it from."

"Oh, no," Ben said. "It doesn't. I bought it for you."

"So, you can flip my skirts over my head and have your way with me, in that case."

"No, I can't," he protested. "I like my bed partners willing, and I wouldn't appreciate being taken by that kind of surprise if I was in their position. And, well." He rearranged the gloves on the chair.

If he'd been capable of it, Elora thought he might have blushed.

"I hadn't considered *that* would be happening," he added.

Now it was Elora's turn to feel confused. "You said I was kissable."

"You are and there are other things we can do, including kissing," he said. Something in his expression softened. "I like you a great deal. More than I should."

"Because I'm food to you?"

"No!" he said quickly. "Because I'm not the man you deserve to be with. You should have someone who's kind and caring."

"You're both of those things!"

"Someone who can walk in the sun," he continued.

"Are you really going to argue that you're not good enough for a poor woman who resorted to stealing the silver from her dead uncle's house?"

"No. I'm going to argue that I'm not good enough for a sweet woman who should have had so many more opportunities than she was afforded. Who hides behind a prickly exterior as a defense mechanism."

Shock at his assessment of her had her frozen in place. "You're the son of one of the wealthiest families in England," she said. "You have two business dynasties behind you."

"And they're worthless to me now, given that I no longer walk among the living. But you do."

Had she inadvertently talked him out of the amorous mood he'd been in at Covent Garden? Why was *he* speaking of himself like he was nothing? Indignation bloomed in her, as bright as the evening dress she still wore. "I will not listen to you speak badly of yourself. So, you're unable to walk in the sun. Plenty of people don't, whether it's bad for their constitution or irritates their skin."

"I believe sunlight is recommended as good for the constitution."

"Not for everyone," she insisted. "We're all different and I'm not going to let a little thing like your sun intolerance be the excuse that stands between us."

"I don't want to destroy you," he said quietly.

"Why not? I have no prospects. I have no suitors and until you kept me from falling backward down the stairs the night we met, I never missed having a suitor."

"Am I a suitor now?"

"Damn it!" she said, stomping her foot. The motion coaxed a smile to his face. "You kissed me on a romantic hot air balloon ride? Yes, that makes you my suitor! That's exactly the kind of thing suitors do!"

"I do love it when you curse."

"You kissed me on a fucking hot air balloon ride. That means something to a girl."

"To me, too."

"You said you wanted to go with me wherever I decided to settle down," Elora said. "I think we should clear the air before I buy a little cottage for us." An awful thought struck her. "You *do* want to stay with me, don't you?"

"How many times do I have to tell you that I do?" he said. Irritation laced his words and he paced the length of the room, an anxious gesture she hadn't seen from him yet. "Please look at this from my perspective. I'm not worrying about ruining you until the societal sense. I don't want to hurt you physically." He paused in front of her, so close she could see the gold flecks in his irises. His eyes were still remarkably human. As was the rest of him, albeit in a different form.

"You won't hurt me. And why are we fighting about this? Are we even fighting?"

"I'm trying to explain that I'm not pushing you away because I don't care for you. I haven't had intimate relations with a human since I was turned. I don't always know my own strength *and*." His expression softened and longing filled his voice. "I meant it when I said you deserve a better man."

Elora didn't care about that. "There's no better man for me than you."

Taking a deep breath for courage, she kissed him, putting as much into it as she did in the hot air balloon.

Ben's response was immediate. His hands reached for her hips and held her against him, fingers bunching up her dress, as Elora's circled his neck. A small gasp escaped her, and he took advantage of it to slip his tongue in her mouth, a motion that made her weak in the knees.

Every cell in her body screamed that there were too many layers between them. Her skin felt hot and tight, like it couldn't contain the rest of her body. She would have plucked at Ben's shirt buttons but she didn't know how to do that gracefully, or if the action would be well-received. So, she kept on kissing him and let her hands explore the back of his neck, his hair. Tiny pinpricks of pain at her lips had both of them pulling away, even though the feeling was starting to feel familiar to Elora.

"Sorry," Ben said.

"Don't be," she replied. She touched her lip and pulled away her finger to see a bead of bright red blood at the tip. Ben looked at her hungrily, and she held it out to him like a treat. He took it and licked it away, his eyes never leaving hers. "I don't think you were that sorry," she said, unable to control the breathiness in her voice.

"I'm trying to control it. I'm getting better at it." His fangs retracted.

"It's all right." She reached for his hands and clasped them, his cool skin a contrast to hers that felt like it was in front of a fireplace. "What happens next?"

He answered her question with another searing kiss, hand toying with her dress's neckline and traveling down along her body. The motion drew a moan from her and she finally pulled at his shirt's buttons, unfastening a few before Ben broke their kiss. He pressed his forehead against hers, his breath coming fast. "Turn around."

The authority in his voice brooked no argument, not that Elora would have offered it anyway. She obediently turned, and his fingers deftly began plucking at the row of buttons on the back of her dress, flicking them apart one by one. He'd helped her button up the dress earlier in the evening, too but it had been nothing like this.

Ben pushed the sleeves off her shoulders, then the garment down her hips.

Elora stepped out of it with more grace than she thought she had at the moment. She couldn't help feeling a little relief when Ben neatly draped it over the back of the chair to join the gloves, taking care to keep something she really loved as it should be.

The dress was forgotten when he turned back to her with a hungry look, one that didn't tell her he was only after her blood. "Your corset."

"Do you want to take it off?"

His raised eyebrow told her he would, and she turned around again. He made short work of her corset laces, pulling the garment apart. This time, Elora helped and tossed it to the floor, not caring where it landed.

She stepped out of her shoes, then stood before him in her shift and stockings. Shyness flashed over her but disappeared just as quickly when he reached out to play with her shift's shoulder strap. "Can I see you? I think I'm a little underdressed for this soirée right now."

Ben's fingers hovered over his shirt buttons. He waited a couple of seconds before speaking. "I'm not making love to you tonight."

Elora's nose involuntarily wrinkled. "Please don't use that term."

"I'm trying to be polite."

"Please don't be. Just because I'm a virgin doesn't

mean you have to use euphemisms with me. I'd prefer it if you didn't," she added.

"Duly noted and while we won't be having sexual relations tonight, I should tell you I've never done anything of this sort with a virgin."

"Please don't tell me about the others. I know they exist, but don't tell me, and please don't use the term 'sexual relations,' either. It sounds like something one would read about in the penny press."

"Congress," Ben said. He pushed aside some of her curls that had slipped out of her hairstyle and pressed a cool kiss to her neck.

It nearly made her forget about the topic at hand. "What do you mean by 'congress'?"

"Penny papers would use the term 'sexual congress.'"

"Oh, God," she moaned.

"Is that from my attempts at being polite or this?" To illustrate his point, he nipped lightly at the skin below her ear, a spot Elora hadn't known was so sensitive until then.

"Both." Her hands scrabbled in his shirt's fabric, plucking at the buttons, desperate to feel his skin against hers.

He helped her, finally shucking it off and leaving it somewhere on the floor.

He guided her to the bed, the backs of her legs hitting the mattress. She hauled herself to the center, her shift bunching up around her thighs as she did.

Ben joined her, crawling on his hands and knees across the mattress with a feline grace. His fingers traced along her stocking to her drawers, his eyes never leaving hers, asking silent permission.

Breathless, she nodded.

He unrolled her stockings from her legs.

The light touch of his fingertips against her skin drawing goosebumps over her body. He angled himself over her, hands holding him up on either side of her head, and lowered his to kiss her. She should have felt claustrophobic, but she didn't. Instead, she buried her fingers in his hair to keep him closer to her until he gave in and gently lowered himself against her. He kissed a trail down her throat, only stopping when his fangs lightly scraped against her neck.

He raised his head. "Sorry," he whispered. The word came out a little strained, like he was fighting some instinct threatening him.

"It's all right. You can bite me if you want."

He hesitated. "No."

He closed his eyes, and it wasn't until his fangs retracted that Elora realized what he was fighting against. Once they receded, he resumed kissing her, head dipping down to her collarbone while one of his hands played with her chemise's strap, sliding it down her shoulder. The worn, thin fabric easily slid down her skin, revealing the swell of her breast, and he pushed aside the other strap, pulling the garment down her body. Bared to the waist in front of him, her skin prickled with awareness, and any shyness she might have felt evaporated under Ben's appreciative gaze.

His lips met hers again, this kiss more demanding than the others before it. Still carefully balancing his weight against the bed so as not to fall on her, his chest lightly brushed against her bare upper half, teasing her already sensitized nipples.

Elora never would have suspected such a small, fleeting gesture would have such an impact, but it did. Desire threaded through her, pulsing and insistent. A moan escaped her.

Ben's head dipped lower and he circled her nipple with his tongue before taking it in his mouth.

This time, Elora cried out and her whole body twitched. Ben's right hand gripped her hip as if steadying her beneath him. He gently massaged her there, working his way down her leg, as he lavished attention on one breast, then the other.

His hand pulled at her drawers, and Ben's eyes met Elora's. "May I?" he asked softly.

She nodded. "Yes." She helped him slide them down her legs, her heart pounding so hard she thought Ben must be able to hear it. He surprised her when he pressed his lips to her inner thigh. She had a good idea of what he wanted to do. Hoping her suspicion was correct, she nodded again.

She was.

He put his mouth on the center of her, where her body ached for him the most.

Her hips bucked and she let out a sharp cry. "Please," she said in a half-sob.

He lifted his head. "Please, what?"

"Please, *everything.*"

"I'm not giving you everything yet," Ben said. "But I'll make this good for you." He moved his head back to where she wanted and needed it, drawing another mewling cry from her.

She could feel her climax already building, as unrelieved tension had her body feeling tight as a wire stretched taut, ready to snap. She grabbed Ben's hair when she did and didn't try to hide her pleasure as it slammed into her. Ben didn't stop until she was wrung out and boneless against the bedcovers.

When he lifted his head again, his fangs had extended again. "Can I bite you?" he asked.

She remembered the first and only time he did it and wondered what it would feel like when they were heaped on a bed together. "Yes."

"Here," he said, swirling a finger on her inner thigh. "Can I bite you here?"

Her breath caught. Intrigued by the idea, she repeated, "Yes."

He moved so quickly she barely felt his fangs pierce her skin, and she felt another climax start to build in her. Ben's fingers took over as he fed from her, sliding in and out of her body in an imitation of what she wanted him to do. She found her second release again as Ben lifted his head, licking the last few drops of blood from his lips.

CHAPTER 11

*B*en could tell Elora was trying to be as quiet as possible as she darted about their room. He could sense that the sun had gone down and night was falling over London. He waited, listening to her tiptoe along the plush carpet, and wondered how she had spent her day. He heard a thump and a muttered, "Fuck," and grinned. It was time to stop making her fumble around in the dark. He lowered the bedcovers from his face. "Good evening."

"I hope I didn't wake you." A lamp flashed on and Ben involuntarily closed his eyes. When he forced them open again, he spotted Elora fumbling with the buttons on her navy blue dress, the same one she'd worn the night they met.

"You didn't at all." He sat up and watched her, lust roaring in his body as he took in the spectacle. "Were you planning on making my wake-up call a little more exciting than usual?"

She looked up from the buttons. Color rose in her cheeks. "Not exactly. I just thought that since… well, you've seen everything anyway, it wouldn't matter if I changed my clothes here instead of the bathroom."

"What for?"

"Aren't we seeing your family tonight? You promised your brother last night, remember?"

Ben did, and he flopped back on the pillows as the memory came back to him. The only thing he wanted to think about from the night before was how Elora sounded and looked as she came.

"I did," he said and squeezed his eyes shut as if he could block out his promise. "God damn it, that was a stupid thing to do, but it was necessary."

"I thought you missed them."

"I do, but I didn't intend to see them again. How am I going to explain it when I don't eat dinner?"

"You could try," Elora suggested. Her buttons unmoored from their fastenings, she slipped out of the dress and hung it up. She picked up a package Ben hadn't seen before and opened it.

"What's that?" he asked, momentarily distracted. He watched as she picked apart the ribbons wrapped around the box.

"I sold everything from Uncle Frederick's house today," she said brightly. "I got more than I expected, too. So, I decided to indulge a little, since I never get to." She removed an aubergine-colored dress trimmed in matching lace along its collar from the box and held it against herself. "What do you think? I bought it at the same pawnshop I always go to. Mr. Boyle even took a couple of shillings off the price for me."

"Who's Mr. Boyle?"

"The owner. He's a nice fellow. I met his son today for the first time. He's training the boy to run the shop when he gets older." She gazed at herself in the room's looking glass, a contented smile on her face.

Ben saw in that one glance that she really hadn't had many opportunities to treat herself, and how much she loved the dress for what it meant: freedom. A chance to start over. "It's beautiful," he said. "And you'll look beautiful wearing it."

Elora gave him a contented smile and started dressing. "We should leave soon."

Her words reminded him of what they'd started to talk about before she opened the box. "I'm not going to be able to eat supper," he warned her. "I had some of your wine that time at Thorn House, but that's it. I can drink some fluids, but too much and anything else makes me ill."

Elora started buttoning her dress.

Ben got out of bed and immediately crossed the room to help her, wanting to be as close to her as possible. She gasped, but he hardly took any notice of it.

"You're naked," she said, but she didn't sound scandalized. Instead, she looked intrigued even as a blush tinged her cheeks.

He looked down. "I suppose I am."

"I've never seen you naked before. You weren't naked when I went to sleep last night."

"I waited until you got out of bed in the morning."

"Weren't you wearing nightclothes to bed at Thorn House?"

"That was in case I had to quickly flee," he explained. "I told you I'm not much of a flyer. I need my legs to escape a bad situation. A running man may attract a few raised eyebrows but will generally be left alone. A *naked* running man is a whole other situation." The buttons in place, he cocked his head at her. "I wish you would've stayed in bed longer. You need your sleep."

"I was fine," she protested.

"You were fine today but you can't be running about day and night. I'm not trying to tell you what to do, I'm reminding you that your health is important. I'd rather you enjoy the daylight, anyway." A pang went through him when he remembered that he would never walk in the sun again.

"I'll have time to rest when I buy that cottage," she said. There was a dreamy note to her voice, one Ben hadn't heard before. Selling her uncle's silverware and jewelry, having the money in hand, must have made her vision a little closer to reality. "Oh, I know what you'll tell your parents!"

Ben waited expectantly.

Elora looked him up and down. She cleared her throat and looked at his face. "Sorry."

"No need to be." He returned to the bed and sat in it, draping the sheet over his lap.

"You told your family you were in Europe. Well, you'll tell them you were being treated for an unknown disease."

"One that keeps me from eating supper?"

"Yes! You suddenly developed reactions to every kind of food you tried, and you've been subsisting on water and, I don't know, bread crusts, for the last year. You didn't want to worry them," she continued. "So, you took it upon yourself to seek treatment in secret. Your malady is mysterious but it isn't contagious, so your family shouldn't have to worry about catching it from you." She beamed. "What do you think?"

It was insane, but it was the best idea Ben never thought of. "I like it."

"We just have to figure out how you met me. They'll want to know all about your fiancée."

There was that. Ben had forgotten that he introduced Elora as such.

"That's simple," he said. We met in an Italian gallery. George and Josephine are expecting us to return to Italy any day anyway."

"But who am I?"

"I don't see why we can't use the truth. You're a duke's niece."

"I'm a duke's sister."

"Right. You've been traveling around Europe with friends because you're unbothered by gossip and convention," he said. "We immediately fell in love and you're determined to see me back to health."

"Which makes us a perfect match."

"It does." In that instant, Ben desperately wished their made-up story was true. He could picture it all. He would have been casually strolling through La Galleria Nazionale when he spotted a head of wild, curly dark blond hair pinned away from the face of a beautiful woman pretending to hide her shock at a nude marble figure with her fan. Like every other he'd had about their meeting, it was an impossible fantasy. "Would you like me to get dressed?" he asked.

"I'm not sure how to answer that," she replied. "I've never seen you without your clothes before, but I don't think this is the time to explore that." She crossed the room, peering into the looking glass and adjusting her hairpins. "And your family will be expecting us soon."

Trepidation had Ben's fingers tightly laced through Elora's during the steam cab ride to his family home in Mayfair. Longing filled him when he thought about the family he never expected to see again, and how much he missed them.

I dearly hope I'm not making a terrible mistake tonight.

He would never forgive himself if he led other vampires to his family. He would sooner wait for the sun to rise and take himself out that way, if Louis or one of his friends didn't stake him first.

Elora leaned over and whispered in his ear, "I've never asked or noticed. Can you see your reflection in the mirror?"

"Yes."

"Could you have your photograph taken?"

Her breath tickled his ear and set off his senses on high alert. He remembered last night and had to fight to keep his fangs retracted. "No one's taken my photograph since I was turned and I've never thought to ask another…" He remembered the driver, who was perched on a seat outside the cab. Ben didn't know how much he could hear through the vehicle's open vents and windows. "Another person like me," he finished. "Although I can't touch any of those things, because of the silver in the photography process."

"Was that a rumor people like you started to throw people like me off your trails?"

"Possibly." Ben hadn't considered it.

I really am a terrible vampire. Just over a year into his change, he still didn't know which vampire myths were rooted in reality and which weren't.

If his heart still beat, it would be loud enough for Elora and the driver to hear. He breathed deeply and tried to think about how happy it would make him to see his parents again, tried to force himself to relax.

The family home looked just as he remembered it, lights in almost every window shining. The same pair of stone lions stood sentry on either side of the front door, contented half-smiles carved into their faces. Ben paid the driver and offered his elbow to Elora when they alighted from the vehicle, guiding her up the front steps. The door opened before Ben could knock, revealing his oldest niece, six-year-old Beth. Her mouth split in a huge grin, revealing a couple of gaps where her baby teeth had fallen out. Perhaps this meant he wouldn't be bitten tonight.

"Mummy!" she yelled over her shoulder. "Uncle Benjy's here!"

Elora turned to him with an amused smile. "Benjy?"

"Short for Benjamin."

"I assumed so, but it's still adorable."

It was on the tip of his tongue to tell her that Beth liked to bite for the sake of it, but he didn't. Hopefully, Beth and her little sister had grown out of the biting stage.

Elora pulled on his arm, encouraging Ben to step over the threshold, but he didn't move. He couldn't walk through the doorway; this wasn't his house anymore. He'd moved out of the family home a year before he was turned, taking up residence in a bachelor's flat in Pimlico.

Elora shot him a horrified look as realization dawned over her. Just as quickly, she recovered. "Hi, sweetheart," she said to Beth. "I'm Elora, Uncle Benjy's fiancée."

Footsteps sounded through the house. Ben was desperate to get inside before adults arrived and wondered what the hell was going on.

"You're going to be a lady when you grow up," Elora continued. She must have picked up on Ben's panic because her words quickened. "It's important for a lady to invite people into the house. Could you do that for us, love?"

Beth looked at Elora like she had just sprouted a second head, but said, "Please come in, Uncle Benjy."

They stepped through the doorway just as Ben's

parents arrived in the foyer, his mother holding her arms out to him. Tears shone in her eyes as she said, "Welcome home."

~

To Elora's relief, Ben's family accepted his story about being stricken with a mysterious illness that kept him from eating anything at supper. She was still too nervous to do much other than pick at her plate, which was a shame since it was among the best food she'd eaten in years, comparable with the meal she had at The Savoy's restaurant. Thankfully, Ben was peppered with questions about his alleged convalescence, and she was largely left alone to force bits of roasted beef into her mouth.

I wonder if it would be terribly rude if I asked to take this home with me?

She answered herself just as quickly. *Inexcusably rude and unbecoming of a duke's sister.*

She still hadn't told Ben everything about Peter's treatment of her, fearing she would never stop talking about her anger if she did so. Likewise, he hadn't told her why he killed Angelique. Curiosity itched at her, but it would have to wait for another time, perhaps after she had purchased that cottage.

If he stays with me.

She still wasn't certain he would want to for the long term. Vampires lived far longer than humans did; forever meant something entirely different.

Do I want to stay with him forever?

A large part of her did, which was unbelievable to her. Her life had been so transient for so long that she never let herself imagine settling down with someone.

"Elora?"

The voice of Katherine Lang, Ben's mother, pulled her out of her ruminations. Elora looked up and hoped she didn't look flustered. "Yes?" She took a quick bite of rosemary-dusted potatoes. "Please pass my compliments to your cook."

Katherine smiled. "Ben told me you two met in an art gallery in Rome, in front of a questionable statue. Are you an artist?"

"Oh, no," Elora said. "Not in the least but I appreciate art." That was the truth. Elora thought if she had more opportunities to do so, she could become quite the patron of fine arts.

"Well, if one can't draw figures, they can at least be grateful to those who do." George Senior, Ben's father spoke up as a servant refilled his plate with a few more slices of roast beef. "Ben tells us you're a duke's sister."

Elora nearly choked on the wine she was sipping but maintained her composure. She had hoped that the subject of Peter wouldn't come up, since it would be difficult to explain their estranged relationship. "I am," she said. "My brother is the new Duke of Wexfield. He's currently traveling."

"It seems wanderlust runs through both of you," George Senior said, and chuckled at his words.

Katherine lightly swatted his arm before silently nodding at the servant to take away her plate. Was it the word 'wanderlust' that she objected to? Or her husband's loud voice?

Elora didn't care about either; Ben's father had a booming voice that carried through the dining room but he was pleasant enough, and clearly moved by his prodigal son's return. With a fiancée, no less. "It does," Elora said, nodding. "Although I don't know where Peter is at the present. The last I heard, he was in Geneva."

"Ah, the Swiss," George Senior said. "The finest watch-makers in the world—Katherine, George, don't look at me like that. I can appreciate the quality of our competitors without being rude about it. The Swiss make damn fine…"

That earned another warning look from Katherine.

Elora smiled.

"Excellent watches and clocks," George Senior finished. He cleared his throat. "Excellent quality. Hand-made. They'll never be automated in the mountains."

"My grandfather had a Lang Timepiece," Elora said. "It's mine now. It still runs perfectly after all these years."

George Senior puffed up with pride and ate another mouthful of beef.

"It's how we met," Ben said suddenly. "It was the point of conversation."

Elora leaned back in her seat and waited for him to continue. "I think we'd all like to hear that story."

"Please do," Katherine exclaimed. "All you've told us is you met in front of an indecent marble statue."

"What do you mean by 'indecent'?" The voice belonged to Ben's nephew, five-year-old Edmund.

"'Indecent' means it isn't for children, darling." Josephine reached over to her son's plate next to hers and cut up a piece of meat. "Two more bites of beef, and then you're done. Beth, stop."

Ben and Elora looked over just in time to see Beth standing behind Ben, bent over, mouth open to… Elora didn't know.

"Is she still biting?" Ben asked.

Josephine sighed and nodded. "It isn't as bad as it used to be," Josephine said. "Nell's stopped it altogether." She nodded at her youngest daughter, sitting in a tall chair, delicately placing peas in her mouth with her fingers, one at a time. Nell didn't look up from her food. "We're still working on her table manners," Josephine added, but she didn't correct Nell's lack of utensil usage.

Elora supposed that it was simply easier to let her eat with her hands if it meant getting food into her.

"Tell us about Elora's watch," George Senior reminded Ben.

"Yes," Ben said. "I was coming back to it. She was standing in front of the statue, pretending that she was scandalized because that's how nice English ladies behave in front of such artworks, and she pulled out her watch to check the time." He smiled and reached for Elora's hand. "Of course, I had to introduce myself."

"And you were all alone?" Katherine said, raising an eyebrow. The gesture reminded Elora of Ben, and she could see who he inherited the expression from.

Elora nodded. "Yes. I've been traveling mostly on my own. Sometimes I meet with my friends or acquaintances along the way."

She held her breath. The Langs were anything but stodgy and traditional, far unlike the aristocratic circles Peter would be running around in these days, but there was still common propriety to be had between those social spheres. One of those rules was that unmarried women didn't travel alone.

Katherine and Josephine didn't appear to care about that. If anything, they looked intrigued by the notion that Elora wandered the globe alone, and for a few seconds, she desperately wished all of it was true.

"How fascinating," Katherine said. "I would have loved to have done that when I was your age."

George Senior swallowed his last bites of meat before speaking. "You still can. The world is your oyster. I'll arrange a tour of wherever you want to go, love."

"I mean, traveling when one is young," Katherine explained.

"Nonsense. You're as young as you ever were."

"No, I'm not."

"We aged like wine, my darling. You're the finest Bordeaux England could ever produce."

That comment earned suppressed smiles from everyone present at the table, but no one commented on it.

"It's different for Elora," Josephine said, "Because she doesn't have the same responsibilities yet that we have." She smiled at Elora from across the table. "It must be such a gift, doing whatever you want when you still can."

Elora exhaled a shaky breath she hadn't known she was holding. She knew a great deal of their tolerance for her alleged gallivanting around the world was due to her social status, as a duke's sister was an excellent catch for a wealthy young man whose fortunes came from industry. It was a shame she wouldn't be able to provide an inroad to the society circles merchants were often denied.

But is it really? Aristocrats are snakes in the grass. The Langs are too kind and friendly to fit in with them.

"It is," Elora said in response to Josephine's remark.

The servant returned to clear George Senior's plate. The family patriarch tossed his linen napkin on the table and leaned back in his chair. "Ben, how did you propose?"

Ben and Elora shared a split-second, panicked look. Both of them had forgotten to create an engagement story. "Why don't you tell it?" Elora asked sweetly.

"Yes," Ben stammered. "Well. I knew from the second I saw her that she was special." He swallowed and pretended to take a sip of wine from the glass in front of him. "I knew after speaking with her that I wanted to marry her."

That comment earned coos from Katherine and

Josephine. Beth, now seated next to her father, rolled her eyes.

"It wasn't as planned or practiced as George's proposal to Josephine was," Ben said. "It was rather spur of the moment."

A strange quiver took hold in Elora's stomach, and with it, longing for something that would never happen.

"We were on a walk around Rome," Ben continued. "I'd been consulting with my doctors about my condition, and…"

Katherine interrupted. "I still can't believe you didn't say anything about your illness."

"I didn't want to worry you, Mother," Ben said. "I'd spent the day in appointments with the doctors. Elora was so kind as to wait for me and be at my side as we flitted around Italy and Spain and France and back to Italy, and I knew we were right for each other." He smiled fondly at Elora, who remained pinned in her seat, riveted by Ben's fiction and wishing it was all true.

"We were wandering about Rome one evening," he said. "And we came upon the Spanish Steps and just talked about what life would be like in England if either of us permanently returned, and I just asked her to marry me. The timing seemed perfect and she said yes."

Josephine sighed, a dreamy look on her face. George, Ben's brother, looked impressed.

"I must say, I never thought you would tie the knot at this age," George said. "Elora, I don't know if he's told you this, but…"

"Please don't," Ben said wearily.

"I already know Ben was something of a hellion before his illness," Elora said. "And I don't care." She tried to make her tone as light and jovial as she could. "After all,

I've been traveling alone for months. I'm just as much of a scandal risk as he is."

Her attempt at humor worked, and her remark drew smiles from the adults around the table. George and George Senior gave her approving looks.

"This is wonderful news," George said. "Marriage will suit you well, Ben." He held up his wine glass. "To Elora, for her willingness to take our prodigal son on in marriage."

Everyone else raised their glasses, and Ben gave her a look of such caring and tenderness that it made her heart hurt.

THE EVENING AIR was mild when they left the Langs' home a few hours later. Ben and Elora walked arm in arm along Mayfair's immaculately maintained streets. Enough people still walked about at half-past ten to make Ben feel safer with Elora at his side, knowing vampires wouldn't swoop in with so many witnesses. He still kept an eye out for a passing steam cab to take them back to The Savoy. They would move on in a day or two, although Ben wasn't sure where. He didn't feel it was a good idea to settle in an English cottage just yet, not while Louis and his friends were still out for blood over Denis's disappearance.

Then there was Angelique's death.

Ben would be forgiven for that if what Louis said back at Thorn House was true, but it was still poor manners for vampires to kill their own. He didn't want to think about Angelique or Denis tonight. "You were magnificent," he said, and pressed a kiss to her temple. She smelled as good as she ever did and he breathed deeply over her hair.

"So were you. I can't believe we didn't think of an engagement story."

"I've never had to concoct lies on the spot like that."

"Really? Given what you've told me of your life before you were turned, I'm surprised."

Ben shrugged. "I lived independently and didn't have to answer to anyone for my actions. I was a bit of a scoundrel, but I wasn't cruel or violent. I didn't have to lie to cover for my misbehavior."

"In front of the Spanish Steps. That's a hell of a story."

"It was the first thing that came to mind and the easiest thing for us to remember if the subject comes up again. Have you been there?"

"I've never left England."

"Instead of the cottage, perhaps we could travel instead."

She stopped on the street to gawk at him. "How?"

"First class travel aboard a dirigible," he replied. "Those cabins are private and windowless or you can stow me away in a trunk. It's certainly possible. "And we aren't without funds," he added. "You don't have to rely solely on the money you received from your pawned things to get us by."

"I would have taken in sewing," she said, and leaned against his shoulder. "That's how I supported myself before I met you."

"You don't have to unless you want to." They passed a row of shops, closed for the night, their windows dark. As they walked by an alleyway, an unmistakable snarl and the coppery smell of blood hit Ben's nostrils and he stopped. "Fuck," he muttered.

Elora's body stiffened and she tightened her hold on his arm. "What is it?"

"It's a vampire." Part of him desperately wanted to flee, but another, more responsible part of him wouldn't be able to live with himself if an innocent human was being devoured in the alley. He looked Elora straight in the eye, hoping she would listen to him. "Stay here." He bolted down the alley with the inhuman speed he'd acquired since he was turned, until he reached the source of the noise. It took a few seconds for the sight to before him reconciled with his mind.

A couple, a man and woman, wearing the height of aviator fashion was pressed against a brick wall. Both wore matching dark brown leather coats, with flight goggles perched atop their heads. The man's head was thrown back in an unmistakable sign of ecstasy as the woman's mouth was pressed against his throat, her suckling sounds an echo that bounced along the building walls to Ben's enhanced hearing.

What the hell?

They were clearly together. Their matching outfits appropriate to dirigible or ornithopter travel testified to that. The man was obviously a human and enjoying the woman's attentions, and she didn't look like she was trying to tear his throat out. Ben wasn't sure what to do. So, he cleared his throat. "Ahem."

She immediately pulled her face away from his neck. Blood ringed her lips and dripped from her fangs. Her pupils dilated until her irises nearly disappeared, and she said, "You won't remember this. Leave us."

Ben's fangs extended when he willed them to.

The man stepped back. "Fuck!" he yelped, echoing Ben's earlier sentiment.

Ben took a couple of steps back, to show he wasn't a threat.

"I'm hers," the man said. His accent placed him as

having Irish origins, although Ben wasn't adept at differentiating between the regions. "You can't have me."

"I don't want to," Ben said. The woman reached behind herself, probably for a stake she had hidden on her person. "I'm not here to eat anyone. I heard you and worried about your safety."

"What?" The woman tilted her head, confused.

"I was walking with my fiancée," Ben replied, maintaining the fiction he created for his family. "And I thought I heard a vampire attack in progress. So, I came here to help, but it appears this wasn't an attack at all, was it?"

"Fiancée? Don't vampires usually keep pets?" the woman asked. She licked blood from her lips and retracted her fangs.

"Ben?" called Elora down the alley. "Is everything all right?"

"Everything's fine," Ben said. "I think."

"Whoever it is, could you tell them I'm not a pet?"

"I think you can come here and tell them that yourself," Ben said. To the couple, he asked, "Can she?"

They both nodded. Ben looked away while they adjusted their flight clothes. Now, he felt a little bad interrupting… whatever he had just interrupted.

Elora scampered down the alleyway to meet them. Even though the couple wasn't a danger to her, Ben still clutched her hand.

"For future reference," the woman said, her voice lightly accented, "When a vampire asks another vampire if a human is a pet, play it safe and always say yes. Other vampires won't infringe on what they see as others' property."

"They." Not "we." *Interesting*.

"Are you her pet?" Elora asked the man, who was adjusting a scarf around his neck to hide his bite mark.

"No," he replied. "I'm her blood mate."

The pair exchanged an affectionate glance before turning back to Ben and Elora.

Ben was reminded of something Angelique mentioned to him shortly after she turned him. Something he'd mentioned it to Elora once. "You're the couple," he said. "The vampire and human. My creator told me about you."

"Who was your creator?" the woman asked.

"She went by the name Angelique."

Her eyes narrowed. "About my height, bright red hair, especially cruel?"

Ben nodded. "Yes."

She surprised him when she stuck out her hand. "Angelique turned me, too. I suppose that makes us siblings of a sort. I'm Emmanuelle. This is my blood mate, Thomas."

"Ben Lang. This is my friend, Elora Stone."

Elora's breath caught when he introduced her as his friend, but she didn't comment on it.

Emmanuelle's gaze flicked between the pair of them. "Where's Angelique?" she asked. "I haven't been able to sense her presence since we arrived in London."

Elora's grip on his hand tightened, and Ben dearly hoped he hadn't just sentenced both of them to death for what he was going to have to admit.

Let's get this over with.

"She's dead. Truly dead," Ben announced.

"Some good news, then," said Thomas. He adjusted his scarf and tucked the ends into his flight coat.

"You're not upset?"

Emmanuelle shrugged. "She was a monster among monsters. I'm not sorry to hear she's gone. Do you know what happened?"

"I killed her."

Thomas and Emmanuelle's eyes widened in surprise, and her face broke out into a smile. "That calls for a celebration," she said. "Would you two like to accompany us back to our dirigible for refreshments?"

ALL OF THEM were quiet in the steam cab that left them at the Vauxhall Airfield. Telegraph poles reached further into the sky than Elora had ever seen. Platforms rose and fell as flying machines landed and took off. The place was teeming with people at this late hour: uniformed workers and tired travelers alike. Stalls sold replacement ornithopter parts and tools, goggle sets, food and drink, luggage, and full sets of clothes, some fashions Elora was unfamiliar with.

"This way," said Emmanuelle, nodding her head to the rented docks. She and Thomas led them to a small dirigible anchored to a platform that was surrounded by a fence that looked to be at least ten feet tall. Emmanuelle unlocked the platform's gate and ushered Elora and Ben through it, then led them up a set of rickety wooden stairs to the dirigible's deck. Its enormous balloon dwarfed the vessel, swaying slightly in the night breeze. A glass-walled box stood in the middle of the deck. On the deck, Thomas removed an enormous ring of keys from his trouser pockets and unlocked the glass box's door. He held it open. "Please come in."

Elora and Ben exchanged a glance.

"It's all right," Thomas said. "Emmanuelle has no intention of eating Elora. We simply wish to talk with you."

Elora hesitated. But a look at Thomas's earnest expression and Ben's tiny nod, she took a deep breath and crossed the threshold with Ben's hand held tightly in hers. He squeezed hers and she felt a little more secure walking into a vampire's lair.

Thomas and Emmanuelle walked in after them, Thomas switching on a pair of lamps. With the strange room illuminated, the top of a staircase was visible, its brass handrail twisting down into the dirigible's underbelly. The vessel's controls were installed in the center of the room, the steering yoke frozen in place by a pair of locks and its levers extended upright. Spotting her curious look, Thomas said, "We decided to enclose the controls when we moved aboard full time. It's no fun at all to be on a dirigible deck in the middle of the night, trying to fly through a storm with the rain in your face. I put in a small furnace and everything." He looked around the glass-walled room with pride.

"It's lovely," Elora said.

Emmanuelle pointed to a pair of chairs nailed to the deck, a small sofa across from them. "Please sit. We have a great deal to talk about, and I'm sure you have questions. Elora, may I offer you tea?"

Elora looked at Ben.

"I don't see why not," he murmured.

"A cup for me too, love," Thomas said. "Please and thank you." He smiled warmly at Elora, his eyes crinkling at the corners, as if to reassure her that it was safe to drink. "It's iced," he added. "We picked it up in America."

It sounded horrid, but Elora wouldn't refuse their hospitality, not if the only other human aboard the dirigible was going to enjoy it, too. She smiled politely when Emmanuelle handed her a sturdy mug filled with cold tea. She sniffed at it. The pleasant aromas of honey and mint greeted her. Tentatively, she tasted it. *Huh. This isn't horrible.*

"Not too bad, is it?" said Thomas, as if he could read her thoughts. He and Emmanuelle took the sofa together, a tight fit. "It's easier than boiling water," he confessed. "We can do it, but it's a pain in the arse to do it more than once a day." He took a deep swallow from his mug. "In fact, I installed…"

"Darling," Emmanuelle murmured. "They aren't here to admire your handiwork."

"Yes, of course," Thomas replied. "My apologies."

Emmanuelle immediately brought the conversation back to where it left off in the Mayfair alley. "Angelique is dead," she said.

Ben nodded. "It was self-defense."

"It was a pity I couldn't get to her first. What happened?"

Ben looked at something outside. Elora tensed, waiting to finally hear what happened to Ben's creator. "She turned me against my will," he said. "Lured me into a room at a, well, gentleman's establishment and fed from me first."

"A common tactic of hers," Emmanuelle said.

"I woke up in a cellar in Wapping," he continued. "I later found out that was one of her favorite hiding places whenever she was in London, I don't know why. She was there and told me what I was, and she brought me to her vampire friends to learn how to be a vampire."

He said the last words with distaste.

Elora thought about Denis and Louis, and the countless others who had to be like them.

"It's one thing to be like this," Ben said. "I've learned to tolerate it but I didn't enjoy being cruel for the sake of it. I still don't. Angelique had such control over me. It felt like she could will me to do what she wanted."

"She could," Emmanuelle said. "Some vampires have

that influence over other vampires. I don't know why or how but she was very old. Perhaps that power develops after being this way for so long."

"I resisted as much as I could," Ben said. "I had to eat and I wanted to do it as easily and painlessly as possible, and Angelique didn't care for my leaving my victims alive and unharmed, with their memories erased of my feeding from them."

Emmanuelle nodded. "She wanted you to hurt them."

"I couldn't bring myself to do it. I spent most of the last year hiding out in abandoned shops and cellars. A few months ago she found me and ordered me to bring her a new toy." He closed his eyes. "She wanted me to go to Madame Tremblay's brothel and find a pretty girl for her. I wouldn't do it and she got angry with me. She threatened me with holy water in a jar, and I killed her with a stake I made myself. I kept it on my person for protection."

"A wise idea," Thomas said. "We always carry them."

"You nearly got me in the alley," Ben reminded him.

"You interrupted us," Thomas said, without a trace of embarrassment. "We decided to see what's changed in London since we were last here, and you know how passion can…"

"Darling," said Emmanuelle. "Not right now. Elora is as red as a beet."

That becoming blush touched her cheeks, but she was hardly red as a beet.

Ben squeezed her hand. "You didn't stake me," he said. "In fact, I came there to rescue you."

"That's a good lad."

"So, you staked Angelique," Emmanuelle said, again steering the conversation in the direction she wanted.

"I did. I wrapped up her remains and dumped them in the Thames. Some of her friends came around to my hiding spot wanting to know what happened to her and I lied and said I didn't know. Then I got out of London."

"She was a sadist. She was also pompous, ill-mannered, and felt entitled to everything in sight," Emmanuelle replied. "Beyond the usual extent for one of our kind. Unfortunately, I spent five years in her company when she turned me, so I am familiar with how she worked. Even for a vampire, she was a monster."

"Where did you meet?" Elora asked. Ben cleared his throat a little, and she realized she may have made a faux pas.

Emmanuelle didn't appear to be affronted. "She turned me in 1799," she replied. "I was a house servant in Brussels. She dragged me around Europe for five years before I convinced her to leave me be."

"And then you two met," Elora said.

Thomas nodded. "About twenty years ago."

"Twenty-one," Emmanuelle replied. She gave his knee an affectionate squeeze.

"Wait." Elora looked at Thomas, who only appeared to be a few years older than her, perhaps his late twenties to early thirties. "Twenty-one years?"

"That's part of the blood bond between us," Emmanuelle replied.

Thomas nodded. "I told you that we're mates."

"How?" Ben asked incredulously.

"Of course, Angelique wouldn't have told you this," Emmanuelle said. "Nor any of the other vampires she communed with. It's not unlike *loup garous*. The werewolves."

"There are werewolves?" Elora shouldn't be surprised, but she was.

"The ones in Britain prefer to be left alone," Thomas said. "They don't leave their home."

"Where are they?"

Thomas and Emmanuelle both shook their heads. "In the north," Emmanuelle replied. "They're a closed society. They stay in their territory and can do as they please there. They don't bother anyone."

Before she could learn more about werewolves in general, British or not, Ben spoke. "What kind of blood bond is this?"

"Vampires can take humans as mates," Thomas explained. "It's protection for the human involved, even if it makes you feel as if you're a piece of meat. Not you, love," he said, looking at Emmanuelle. "I mean with other vampires."

"I know." Emmanuelle's look was equally warm.

"There's a blood swap," Thomas continued. "I didn't care for that. Again, I'm sorry, love, but I don't like drinking blood. It marks humans as untouchable among other vampires. It's our version of marriage."

"And you don't age?" Elora asked. "Unless I'm misunderstanding something?"

"I was twenty-eight when I met Emmanuelle," Thomas replied. "The bond has stopped my aging. I can still go about in the daytime as I please, I can still eat human food, and we've noticed in the last year or two that Emmanuelle can tolerate seeing a sunset without being harmed."

Beside her, Elora thought she noticed Ben's attention latched on to the possibility of seeing the sun again, albeit in small bursts.

"We love each other," Thomas said. "And this works for us."

"How long does it last?" Ben asked.

Emmanuelle and Thomas answered almost simultaneously. "Forever."

CHAPTER 12

*B*en mulled over the new information he'd been given on the steam cab ride back to The Savoy. He had a sister, of sorts and that sister was mated to a human.

While Thomas gave Elora a tour of the dirigible's underbelly, Emmanuelle took Ben aside. She explained a few more things about blood bonds and mates to him, and Ben committed every word to memory. He didn't know what he wanted to do with what she told him, but he hoarded the knowledge, just in case. It was a relief to meet a vampire who was still more human than not. It was a boon to Ben's sanity, a sign that he wasn't destined to turn into Angelique or Denis down the road.

Emmanuelle had been turned nearly a hundred years ago and by her own admission survived on Thomas's blood and didn't tire of it. Her monstrous side had never overtaken her impulses, leaving a trail of death in her wake. She had found a way to make vampirism work for her, and Ben was determined to follow in her footsteps. He helped

JESSICA MARTING

Elora out of the steam cab when they reached the hotel, forever grateful for her presence, her warmth.

"I think tonight went well," she said as they walked through the lobby doors.

"My family likes you."

"I thought so, but I wasn't sure." She bit her lip, a gesture she likely hadn't intended to be as alluring as it was, and continued. "I hope they don't find out about my relationship with Peter, or lack of it."

"I don't think they would care," Ben replied. "If anything, my parents don't have a great deal of regard for aristocrats. I think they were relieved to see you're unconventional."

"The person we pretended I was is unconventional."

The lift door opened. Ben and Elora stepped into the car. They didn't speak again until they were locked in their hotel room.

"I think I could live as Emmanuelle and Thomas do," she said dreamily. "There's something so romantic about traveling the world and seeing everything, whenever you want. Not being tied down. What do you think?"

"What happened to the seaside cottage?"

"There's time for that," Elora said. "I'm just daydreaming, don't worry about it."

He didn't want her to think he was being dismissive of her feelings. "Keep daydreaming and tell me about it. I'll always listen."

She gave him a contented smile that was so sweet it squeezed the place where his heart used to be.

He kissed her, putting everything into it that he could. His body, hyper-conscious of her presence all night, flared to life as it pressed against hers. She gave a startled mewl of surprise but slid her arms around his neck, playing with his hair on the nape on his neck in a way that drove him

168

mad. His fangs extended, reminding him that the taste he'd taken from her the night before wasn't a meal. He immediately pulled away from her, regret filling him, as he unsuccessfully tried to will them away.

Elora seemed to sense what was happening. "Are you hungry?"

He nodded and looked away.

"You can feed," she said shyly. "I don't mind. I like it."

He knew she did, and despite Emmanuelle's assurances that his urges were controllable, he was still afraid of doing something wrong, of hurting the person he now cared about the most in the world. "I want to do more than feed from you," he said, voice rough.

She started unbuttoning her dress. "You can. I want that, too and don't worry about hurting me." She stood up on tiptoe and pressed a kiss to his cheek. "I'll be fine. Have you lost control, ever?"

He shook his head. "Although I've killed some animals out of necessity." He'd told himself at the time that it wasn't dissimilar to eating meat.

"But not people."

"No, only Angelique. I could never bring myself to do that to a human."

Angelique was at first amused, then enraged, at Ben's preference not to kill his victims. His glamouring skills often left something to be desired, but he always managed to erase their minds of him feasting on them. He assumed their disbelief that an actual vampire had fed from them helped him in that regard.

"And you won't with me," said Elora. She slipped out of her dress, then hung it up with care and stopped to admire it for a few seconds.

"You looked lovely tonight," Ben offered. "You still do. But I like seeing you in clothes that make you happy."

She turned shining eyes to him. "Thank you."

"And I don't know about living aboard a dirigible. It wasn't too long ago that you thought a hot air balloon was too high in the air. Let's take a holiday sometime and have a dirigible take us there."

"I'd love that," she said. She curled her hands in his, her warm skin a marked contrast to his cool. "Ben."

She spoke with his name with an urgency he'd never heard before, a sensual note to it that had the hairs on his arms standing on end. "Yes?"

"I don't want to think about the future and all the places we can go after this is behind us. I want to think about the present, with you."

He knew what she was asking, and he wanted the *present* with her, too but there was a danger she kept glossing over. "I haven't done anything sexual since I was turned."

"I haven't had any at all. So, I suppose that puts us on more even footing."

She was wise in so many ways, yet alarmingly naive in others. "That's not what I was worried about. I don't want to tear you apart the way only a vampire could."

"Did you tear people apart before you turned?"

He stared at her, aghast, and not just because she had unhooked her corset and left it on a chair.

She perched on the edge of the bed, waiting for his explanation.

"No," he replied. "Never dreamed of it. That doesn't appeal to me." He sat down next to her, the bed sagging a little under their combined weight.

"What does?" Elora's question was breathless.

What was the best way to explain his preferences to someone he was looking forward to sharing them with, without stuttering the entire time? It would be easiest to be as blunt and to the point as possible. "I like it when my bed partners want to be with me," he said. "I like knowing what they want. I want both of us to feel good."

"Is it important that I don't know what I'm doing?"

He was surprised she would ask such a thing. "Of course not. This isn't watchmaking. Humans have been figuring out sex for thousands of years. It's supposed to be fun," he continued. "For all parties. And if you're wondering if your lack of experience and some vampires' reactions to it factors into how I feel about you, it doesn't. I'd feel the same way and want to spend the night in bed with you as much as I could, no matter what."

She leaned over and lightly nipped his earlobe, surprising him and setting all of his body's responses on high alert.

I suppose I'm not that dead.

Her lips found his, and he smiled against them.

"WHAT IS IT?" Elora asked. She could feel him smile, like he knew something she didn't.

"Just thinking,"

"About what?"

"You," he said. His expression softened. "How being with you made me realize I'm not a monster."

"Just that? You're not thinking about how alluring I am?" She tried to make her tone as sensual as she could, and it had its intended purpose.

Ben's eyes darkened. He took her face in his hands, his kiss insistent and searching.

She dared to reach for his shirt and with shaking fingers, plucked at its buttons. Catching sight of his raised eyebrow, she said, "It just doesn't seem fair that I'm half undressed and you're not."

"Fair point."

He helped her, shucking off his shirt, and watched as Elora briefly struggled with his trouser placket. With them loosened, he guided her back on the bed until she was lying down, then followed suit, propping himself up on his side.

She'd appreciated how he looked the night before but hadn't had any time to explore him as he brought her pleasure. Now she had the opportunity to touch him, explore him, and she wasn't going to waste it. She traced her fingertips over his chest, his skin cool to the touch, letting her hand wander lower. She kept an eye on Ben's expression, wanting to pick up any sign that he was enjoying it, and his rough exhale through gritted teeth told her she was doing something right. Her hand hovered over his open waistband, and she hesitated. "Can I?"

He nodded. "I'd love it if you did."

He helped her push the rest of his clothes down his hips, and then he was lying next to her, completely naked. A powerful rush of lust and curiosity had her looking over his magnificent body, unsure what to do next. She wanted to do everything but had no idea where to begin. Her eye was drawn to his erection but it felt presumptuous to start there. She ran her hands over his hip bones to the tops of his thighs, fascinated at the feel of his skin beneath her fingertips, at his sharp intake of breath.

He wanted this, wanted *her*, as much as she did.

Emboldened by his reaction, she dragged her fingertips over his erection, an experimental touch, curious to see his next response. A low moan issued from his throat, and Elora grinned, a little heady with the power she wielded over him. "Does this feel good?"

"It's an absolute fucking tease," he ground out. He took her hand in his and wrapped it around him, urging her to use more pressure. "Like this."

"You told me you like being teased."

"I do," he said. "I'm thoroughly enjoying this… ah!"

Following his guidance, Elora stroked his length, equally fascinated and aroused by the muscles bunching along his body. His expression was a combination of pleasure and pain. "Do you want me to do to you… what you did to me last night?" she asked shyly. "I'd like to."

"I would, too, but this will be over before it begins if you do that," Ben replied through gritted teeth. "Another time. I want this to be good for *you*."

Elora let him go and slipped out of her undergarments, not caring where they landed on the floor. "It will be."

She leaned over to kiss him, thrilling in the sensation of his skin against hers, with nothing between them. His hands explored her body, his sure, gentle touch sending a bolt of lust straight to her center. She urged him over her and he willingly obliged until she was on her back. His face hovered over hers, eyes searching her as one of his hands lazily stroked her leg.

"You're so beautiful," he said.

She hadn't expected to hear that at the moment, but she liked it. She brushed a lock of dark hair off his forehead. "I thought you were the most attractive man I'd ever seen the night we met." She could have sworn color tinged his cheeks at her words.

"And now?"

"Are you finagling for more compliments?" she teased. "Right now?"

He urged her knees apart and settled his body against hers. "Possibly."

"Even though this is happening?" she said. "All right. I still think you're the most handsome man I've ever met."

He paused at her entrance, waiting to see her reaction. A shiver of anticipation rippled through Elora and she nipped at his lower lip. "Do it."

His fangs extended as he inched forward, and Elora gasped at the unfamiliar, but welcome invasion. His body was tense, his expression strained as he fought to control himself as he eased into her. Instinctively, Elora wrapped her leg around his hips and breathed deeply. "I'm all right," she whispered. "You won't break me."

That was all the encouragement he needed. He pushed forward until he was seated inside her, her body against hers. He remained motionless as Elora adjusted herself, her body learning to accommodate his.

It felt…. Good. Better than she expected. An unexpected wave of affection crested in her as she thought about how important this was to her, how much she enjoyed being as close to Ben as two people could get. *If I think about this too much, I'll cry.* And tears meant Ben would insist on stopping, even if they weren't from pain. She shimmied her hips against him, urging him to move. "I told you. I won't break."

That was all the encouragement he needed.

He withdrew and surged forward again, then gained a solid momentum, a rhythm Elora hadn't known she desperately needed until then. She could already feel a climax building and kissed Ben as it welled inside her.

His fangs nicked her lips, tiny pinpricks of pain, and Ben's tongue licked them away. He buried his face against her neck, and for a second thought he was going to bite her, but he raised his head instead, dark eyes glazed with lust boring into hers.

As her orgasm peaked and Ben's body stiffened against

hers, she forgot there was anyone else in the world but them, that they were safe as they were in that moment. When Ben pulled out of her body and rolled over, taking her with him, she thought this had to be the best place in the world, with the person she loved the most.

Love. She snuggled against him and draped an arm over his chest, content. She would tell him later.

ELORA SIGHED in her sleep and snuggled closer to Ben, who wrapped the blankets around her a little more snugly.

He'd hardly been able to sleep all night. His being a vampire hadn't stopped him from wanting to pretend he was still human, still normal, just for a night with her. She was so *warm.* Had humans always been that warm? Was he like that when he was still alive? He remembered the words Emmanuelle told him when they were aboard her dirigible, her encouragement at his maintaining regular human behavior, no matter what. It was a thin line, she said, between human and monster before vampirism was added into the mix. Then there was the second thing she told him: "Take care of her. She loves you, even if she hasn't said it yet."

Ben didn't know what to think of that.

He could hardly ask Elora. Ben had never been in love before and he hadn't a clue how to bring that up. He didn't want to wake her, and he liked the feeling of her curled up against him, so he stayed put, listening to her deep, even breathing. A few locks of hair fell away to reveal her neck and the healing puncture wound there, a memento from his feeding from her between lovemaking sessions during the night.

Despite the drapes being closed and the bed's curtains

released from their moors on the posts, Ben could tell dawn was approaching, a sense he developed soon after he was turned. Now, he could start to feel himself doze off, and he didn't fight the urge to sleep. He hoped Elora spent the day in the sunshine. He wanted to smell it in her hair when she returned from wherever she wanted to go today. Sunshine and lemon verbena sounded good.

The slightest snick of the door lock being disengaged had Ben wide awake and alert. He pried Elora off him and sat upright, swinging his legs over the side of the bed and pushing the curtain out of his way.

The door opened, and a man and woman stepped inside the room, closing it behind him. He couldn't make out their features in the dark yet, and he blinked, trying to force his eyes to adjust.

"What is the meaning of this?" Ben demanded.

Elora stirred behind him. "Ben?" she said sleepily. "What's going on?"

The man turned on a nearby lamp, revealing himself and the woman to be totally unfamiliar. Both wore dark clothes and the woman had a pair of flight goggles on a strap around her neck. The man had an enormous ring of keys at his waist.

Both had silver chains in their hands.

Oh, this was going to be bad. Very, very bad.

"Stay here," Ben commanded Elora.

"Who are these people?" Elora asked.

Ben had never laid eyes on them before, but he had a good idea as to who had sent them. "Are you here on behalf of Louis?" he asked.

The woman pulled up her flight goggles over her eyes and the man removed a pair from his pocket and put them on. Ben realized they must be a defense against vampire glamour. "We're here on behalf of Louis and Denis," the woman said. Her voice barely contained her anger, and he guessed she had been one of Denis's pets or a familiar.

"Well, you've made a mistake!" came Elora's indignant protest from behind him.

Ben turned around. "Not now," he whispered.

"Why the hell not? Who *are* these people?"

"We can take care of this affair with you being willing," said the man. "Or not. It's your choice."

"What do you mean?" Elora asked. Not caring that she was naked, she tried to push past Ben, who held out his arm to keep her from leaving the bed.

"You're coming with us," the woman said, pinning her gaze on Ben. "And you won't make a fuss about it. Get dressed."

"Or what?" Elora snapped.

"Elora," Ben said urgently, hoping she would finally listen. Damn it, if she would just stay quiet, perhaps these people would forget she was in the room and she would stay unharmed.

But both of the intruders raised small clockwork pistols, aimed squarely at the bed. "These are loaded with silver bullets," the man said. "Lethal to your pet either way."

For once, Elora didn't protest that she wasn't Ben's pet, but it wasn't because she was willing to play along in a life-or-death situation. She shrank back, her terrified eyes on the weapons.

Ben stood up. "I'm getting dressed," he said when he saw they didn't lower their guns. "I'll go with you, but you will leave her alone."

"Dress here," the woman said impatiently.

He was going to anyway because he didn't trust them to be alone with Elora. He quickly dressed in the evening clothes he'd worn last night, creased from their night on the floor but none of that mattered, as long as Elora remained safe.

"It's nearly sunrise," the man said. "Unless you want to cook like an egg on a skillet, you have to hurry."

Ben steeled himself, regret and fear roiling through him. "One moment," he said, holding up his hand to illustrate his point. He returned to the bed, where Elora remained with the sheet pulled up over her breasts, and said quietly, "I'll be fine. Don't worry about me."

Tears leaked from the corners of her eyes and she sniffled. "I should come with you."

"Absolutely not," he said. "I'll get out of this, I always do."

Before she could offer another protest, he kissed her, putting as much passion into it as he could. He had a sinking suspicion it would be their last.

Then he faced the intruders. "Hold out your arms," the woman said.

"Is it necessary to manacle me? I'm cooperating."

Without another word, the pair each wrapped their silver chains around his wrists and locked them. It took a few seconds before the metal had its intended effect on him, and he had to bite the inside of his cheek to keep from screaming. He could smell his flesh burning. But he remained silent as he walked out of the room, flanked on either side by the mysterious pair.

CHAPTER 13

*E*lora could hardly believe what she had just witnessed. But she didn't have to pinch herself to know that it hadn't been a horrible dream.

She nearly vaulted off the bed, taking the bedsheet with her. She followed Ben and the intruders out of the room. "Wait!" she yelled down the corridor. She picked up the bottom of the sheet to keep from tripping and hurried until she reached them. The man pressed the button for the lift, then whirled around with his clockwork pistol trained on her. The woman followed suit.

Elora froze.

"Go back to the room," Ben said. His voice was low and strained, his shoulders trembled in pain. He scratched at his bound wrists, pushing aside his shirt cuff and revealing burned, reddening skin.

She cried out at the sight.

"I don't want to shoot you in the open," the man said. "But I will if I have to."

"Elora, go back," Ben pleaded. "*Please*."

She hated that she had no real choice right now.

The lift gears groaned as the car ascended, perhaps in protest of the early hour. She knew she didn't have much time. Praying they wouldn't shoot either of them, she kissed him for what she hoped wouldn't be the last time. She put everything she could into it, and he did likewise. A sob escaped her and tears slid down her face. The lift doors opened and they were rudely pulled apart. Through her film of tears, Elora couldn't see who did it. When she wiped away her eyes, she could see Ben clearly, and the desolate look on his face.

As soon as the lift closed, she bolted back to their room before anyone saw her wearing nothing but a sheet.

Rage galvanized her into action and she quickly dressed. She couldn't follow them since they had too much of a head start. She also didn't doubt that Ben's captors would make good on their threats of killing her. But she still wasn't going to dally while she thought of a plan. Shoving a few pins into her disobedient hair, she collected her satchel and left the room, locking the door behind her.

She knew exactly one other vampire other than Ben, and she dearly hoped that vampire hadn't taken off with her human lover in their dirigible.

London's version of dawn breaking greeted her when she nearly ran out of The Savoy's front door, the sun trying to peek through sallow gray clouds. As she hurried through the streets, looking for a cab, steam or otherwise, she hoped Ben was protected from it. Hopefully, his captors weren't only going to use anything worse than silver to hurt him.

His eyes had been red-rimmed with pain, trying to keep it under control. Elora had never seen the kinds of burns his wrists bore before he stepped into the lift.

To her dismay, not a single cab appeared on The Strand. Biting back a cry of frustration, she kept marching in the vague direction of Vauxhall Airfield, hoping a cab would meander its way over the street.

The street was eerily quiet, but years of living in London told Elora that she wasn't truly alone at this time of day. She kept an eye out for footpads or other suspicious characters, which forced her to slow down in her mad dash. She wouldn't be of any help to Ben if she tripped and broke an ankle, or if she was set upon by someone intent on stealing her satchel. Or only one of those things. She didn't know which would be worse at that moment. The lack of funds meant she wouldn't be able to pay a driver to take her to Vauxhall Airfield, and the lack of mobility…

"Miss Stone!"

She froze. Who the hell was calling her? She knew no one would who lived around The Strand, and Ben's family was too respectable to be out at this hour. She turned around to see a dapper man walking briskly toward her. It took a moment for her to recognize him. "Sergeant Sloan?"

She hadn't thought of the Liverpool policeman since she and Ben made their mad flight from Wand's Hollow. What the hell was he doing in London? A heavy, ominous ball formed in her stomach, a leaden weight. She had a terrible feeling about this.

"Miss Stone," the sergeant said as he approached her with a friendly smile on his face "This is quite the coincidence."

Something in her snapped. "It certainly is," she said icily. "It's quite the fucking coincidence that you turn up outside the exact hotel I've been staying at, the day my friend is kidnapped. Quite the coincidence!"

He stared at her, agog.

"Am I under suspicion for that murder in Wand's

Hollow? Because I assure you, I had nothing to do with it! I got out of there as soon as I could!"

"What do you mean, your friend's been kidnapped?" There was genuine concern written on his face, as if this piece of information was new to him.

"Exactly what I said!" Elora shouted. Her voice bounced off the tall buildings surrounding them, but she didn't care. "And Ben had nothing to do with the murder, either. Why are you following us? Aren't you supposed to be in Liverpool?"

"Miss Stone, I'm as flummoxed as you are about this kidnapping," Sergeant Sloan said. "I assure you, I had nothing to do with it, and I know you nor Mr. Lang did not kill the Wand's Hollow postmaster."

She waited for him to continue. When he didn't, she said, "Well, who did?" She was wasting precious time. Elora scanned the street, willing a cab to come her way.

"If I tell you, you'll think I'm mad," he finally replied.

"I already do," she snapped. "It's not even half-past five and you're already awake and wandering the street."

"So are you."

"I have a purpose," she said. "I'm trying to find my kidnapped friend."

"Why don't you contact the police?"

"Because this isn't something the police can help with."

As she said the words, understanding dawned on her, brighter than the pale sun struggling to rise through the clouds. It was the same revelation she'd had back in Wand's Hollow, when she questioned why he would be there, investigating the murder. "You're not in London on behalf of the Liverpool police."

He gave her a knowing look, and she knew she was right.

"Are you even a policeman?" she asked.

"I'm really a policeman," he confirmed. "But you're correct. I'm investigating this murder case for personal reasons. Just as you're setting out half-cocked to rescue your kidnapped friend without notifying the police. They would certainly take notice of the kidnapping of the son of a well-known titan of industry."

"You know who Ben is," Elora said flatly.

"I know who you are, too, and that you didn't have permission from the current Duke of Wexfield to be holing up in his country home."

"I'm the duke's sister," she replied. "I have a right to visit a family home."

"Not in this case," Sloan said. "Look, Miss Stone, why don't you tell me where you're going, and I can escort you there? My ornithopter is waiting nearby."

Suspicion again flared in her, hot as a flame. "How can I trust you?"

"Because I suspect we're after the same sort of people," he said. "If not the exact people."

Her breath stilled involuntarily. "Do you know who kidnapped Ben?"

"Not precisely, but I have a very good idea as to who ordered the kidnapping. The next step is figuring out where they're hiding."

Elora was desperate, and she had no choice if she wanted a chance to save Ben. "All right," she said. She dearly hoped she wasn't about to make a deadly mistake for him, or Emmanuelle and Thomas. "I need to get to the Vauxhall Airfield, now."

~

Ben didn't think the burning pain in his wrists could possibly get any worse, but as the minutes ticked by, he was proven wrong.

The stomach-turning odor of burned flesh assaulted every one of his senses, and judging by the way his kidnappers' nostrils flared, they were bothered by the smell, too. As he was forced into the back of a steam cab waiting outside The Savoy, a sizzling sound reached his ears, and it took a few seconds for him to realize it was the sound of his skin cooking under the silver.

Only after the cab's door was closed and locked behind him, a captor on either side of him trapping him in place, did he dare speak. "I'm going to cooperate with you," he said through gritted teeth, trying not to betray his agony. "You don't have to use silver cuffs on me."

"We were ordered to use them," the woman replied, voice soft.

"And I won't tell whoever ordered you to kidnap me that you replaced them with something that won't burn my hands off my arms," Ben said.

Neither of them responded, nor did they remove the chains.

Ben sighed and tried to settle back against the seat and foment a plan of escape, but the space between their bodies was too narrow to do anything but sit with his shoulders hunched in, his body nearly folded over on itself. "Is the driver part of this charade?" he asked a few minutes later.

"Yes," the man said. "Don't try screaming or anything. He won't help you."

A dark awareness prickled at the back of Ben's neck, a warning that sunrise was imminent. "I might not be able to help the screaming," he said. "It's nearly daybreak."

"Damn it," muttered the man. He dug around his

trousers pocket and removed a hood and pair of gloves. Without another word, he draped the hood over Ben's head and neck. The gloves were forced on his hands, over his silver chains.

Ben tried to bite back his pain but an undignified yelp escaped him. "Is it too much to ask your names?" Ben asked. "Or at least who your masters are?"

His only response was silence. The steam cab made a particularly sharp turn, forcing all three of them to shift to the left. "I'm Caroline," the woman said after a few moments.

The man wordlessly growled at him, but she ignored it.

"I served Denis," she continued voice wavering.

Ben guessed at least one of them had served Denis. He didn't reply.

"You killed him," Caroline said, voice rising. "We know you did."

"I didn't," Ben said, which was technically the truth but he would die for Denis's death if it meant Elora was spared. Still, he lied. "I don't know where he is."

Caroline's response was to pull hard on his manacled hands, an unexpected torture that finally made Ben scream.

It felt like his skin was peeling off, and the horrific smell of rotting flesh had his stomach roiling. He didn't know if it was possible for vampires to be physically sick, but if she did that again he would find out for sure.

"You absolute liar!" she screamed. "You *fuck*! Bits of him were left outside that house! You…"

"Not now," said the man in a sharp rebuke. "They want him whole."

"Are you sure about that?" Ben asked. "It feels like these things are going to roast my skin clean off."

185

Caroline jerked the chains again, albeit not as hard, but didn't speak.

The man's response about "wanting him whole" confirmed Ben's suspicions that he was going to be made to suffer whoever ordered his kidnapping killed him.

No. Do not think that way. You promised Elora you were going to get out of this alive. Well, as alive as a vampire can be, and you're going to do that.

Another thought struck him. *I have to tell her I love her.*

This was a devil of a time to realize that.

He desperately wished he'd said the words "I love you" before she drifted off to sleep in his arms. He no longer cared that she was human and he no longer was or that she deserved a man who could walk in the sunshine with her, have children with her. He selfishly wanted to spend the rest of his days and nights with her, living in the little cottage by the sea she envisioned.

He wanted the blood bond Emmanuelle and Thomas shared, the quick exchange of blood that would link them for as long as they walked the earth. He had never pictured a wedding and marriage before he died, but he wanted that now, too. As he suffered in silence, he distracted himself with fantasies of the life he would give anything to share with the brightest and most spirited woman he had ever met.

The steam cab lurched again, this time to the right, and beside him, Caroline let out a ragged sob as she was undoubtedly wading through her memories as Denis's pet.

A brackish smell suddenly filled the air, an odor he probably wouldn't have been able to pick out when he was still alive but was unmistakable to his nostrils. He'd dumped Angelique's earthly remains into the water near here. The steam cab was near the Thames, familiar territory. By the scents around them, they were near Wapping.

The buildings around the dock area were popular with vampires, owing to the transit population and abundance of places to slumber away the day.

The cab slowed down and the odor and heat of coppery steam filled the cab, a telltale sign the vehicle was stopping for good. Its vibrations abruptly ceased, and there was a pause as Caroline and the still-unnamed man unhooked the steam cab's doors to let themselves out.

They had arrived at their destination, and he knew his surroundings. He forgot about the burning agony in his wrists for a few seconds as he realized this leveled the proverbial playing field for him. He knew every nook and cranny of Wapping's hiding places and shortcuts.

He might well get out of this in one piece, after all.

Elora officially didn't care for flying. She decided she hated heights, and another trip aboard a hot air balloon or ornithopter would be too soon.

She hated that she couldn't stop loathing Sergeant Sloan's ornithopter or what felt like the massive distance between the flying machine and the ground while she was on the hunt for Ben. It felt selfish to be terrified for her life right now, clinging to the sergeant's midsection with all her might.

London whizzed past them beneath their feet. If Elora hadn't been scared out of her mind for herself and the man she had fallen in love with, she might have fascinated herself with the sight of the city waking up.

She only screamed once during the journey, shortly after the ornithopter took flight and sailed above the Thames. They had come perilously close to clipping the machine's wings when Sloan flew it a little too near

Tower Bridge, dipping to the side at one point before Sloan righted it with his body weight from the pilot's seat in front of her. Since then, Elora had kept her eyes squeezed shut behind her flight goggles. She breathed deeply through her nose in an attempt to keep herself from vomiting and focused on the wind rippling through her hair and clothes. As it was, her hat barely stayed in place.

If it flew off, she would be damned if she would let go of the sergeant to catch it.

Neither of them had brought up exactly who Sloan was after for the postmaster's death. Elora suspected the policeman knew he was searching for a supernatural creature, but she wasn't going to be the person to confirm the existence of vampires to him. She just needed to get to Thomas and Emmanuelle's dirigible and work from there.

Part of her desperately wanted to tell Sloan exactly what happened to Wand's Hollow, if for nothing else that he could transport her around London far faster than a steam cab or the Underground. The other part didn't know if Sloan would react by killing every vampire he came across, including Ben.

Her stomach nearly dropped out of itself when the ornithopter began its descent, and she forced her eyes open to make sure it wasn't a crash over the river. When she saw docked dirigibles and ornithopters come into view, she was finally able to relax a little.

They'd made it to the airfield.

She waited until the ornithopter touched the ground before she took off her flight goggles. She unwrapped herself from around Sloan's chest and lifted herself off the passenger seat directly behind him with shaky legs. "Thank you," she said, handing the goggles back to Sloan. She looked around the ornithopter's small basket for her missing hat and noticed it was gone, probably long fallen in the Thames.

Oh, well. It didn't matter.

She dug a few notes out of her satchel and handed them to Sloan. "For your trouble," she said. She lifted the basket's door latch and stepped out, never so grateful to be back on land.

Instead of resuming the ornithopter's flight, Sloan removed his own flight gear and locked them away in a box bolted to its floor. "Which dirigible are we visiting?" he asked.

"There's no 'we' from here on out," Elora protested. Hefting her satchel over her shoulder, she turned away.

"There is," Sloan replied, and fell into step beside her. He pushed the money she'd given him back at her.

"I'll thank you not to do that," Elora said icily.

"And I'll thank you to remember that I'm on your side," Sloan retorted. "Before you go running off into an incredibly dangerous situation, you're not prepared for you, will you listen to me?"

Elora stopped walking, only because she was sure he wouldn't have any compunction about grabbing her arm and forcing her to stay in place. If he did that, she would scream and people would come running. Her mission would be delayed. So, she crossed her arms under her breasts and gave the policeman what she hoped was the haughtiest look she could muster.

"I understand time is of the essence here, I really do," said Sloan. "But we're walking into a den of vampires. Don't look at me like that, Miss Stone. I know exactly what your friend is."

His statement confirmed her suspicions, but she still didn't trust him. "How can you be certain?"

"I follow supernatural activity in my spare time. Most

of the beings who live and walk among us leave humans alone and we have nothing to fear from them. Some of them don't. The vampire who killed the Wand's Hollow postmaster wasn't one of the vampires who leave us be."

"Ben didn't do it," Elora said weakly.

"I know that."

"The vampire who did. He's dead. Truly dead. I killed him myself."

Sloan's expression was unreadable under the brim of his hat, and she continued.

"His name was Denis. He turned up at Thorn House the same night I did, when I met Ben. He was hiding out there." There wasn't enough time to go into the specific details of their meeting, so she skipped them. "The point is, Denis nearly killed both of us. I got to him first when he attacked Ben. I did it with a broken table leg. Denis must have killed the postmaster before he tried to attack us at the house." Sloan didn't immediately reply, so Elora forged on. "I'm sure you can understand why I didn't tell you anything."

He nodded. "Do you know who kidnapped Mr. Lang?"

"I don't know their names, but they're familiars or pets or whatever vampires call humans who serve them. I'm sure they were Denis's familiars, or possibly Louis's. He's another vampire who flew to Thorn House after Denis was killed."

"What do you mean by 'flew'?"

"Just that," Elora replied. "Louis can fly. Ben can't. He said he's tried but he was unsuccessful."

Sloan closed his eyes and a muscle in his jaw ticked. Elora had the distinct impression that he was trying to keep from going off on a foul-mouthed tirade in front of a lady and an entire airfield. "I didn't know about their ability to fly," he finally said, voice tight.

"I'll tell you everything I know about vampires if we can just get to the dirigible I need to go to," she said. The sense of urgency and her own frustration at consistently being stymied by the tenacious policeman pulled at her. She had to keep herself from grabbing his hand and taking off in the direction of Thomas and Emmanuelle's dirigible.

"Are you Mr. Lang's pet?"

"What? No."

"You have a fading bite mark on your neck."

Elora touched the spot on her throat that wasn't covered by her blouse's collar and thought of the other bite mark on her inner thigh. "It's not like that. I'm his lover."

The frank admission had Sloan's eyebrows raised.

"Now, may we *please* get to where I need to go? I think they'll have answers for us. Or at least they'll know where to find them."

Finally, Sergeant Sloan nodded.

He followed her as she threaded her way through the airfield docks, each platform holding a dirigible. A few people were visible on their decks or platforms.

Despite Elora's fear that the dirigible she needed to go to would be gone, it was just as she remembered it from the night before. And, every deity Elora could be think of be praised, Thomas stood on its deck, a cup in one hand and a cigarette in the other. Elora stood outside their locked platform gate. "Thomas!" she shouted, and waved. Perhaps a tad dramatic, but her sanity was on edge.

It had the intended effect. Thomas looked down and started. "Fancy seeing you here in the cold light of day," he called.

She had to force herself to keep her voice calm and level. "Could I speak to you? It's important."

He nodded. With his cigarette clamped between his

lips, quickly left the dirigible and descended the platform stairs. He unlocked the gate and ushered them in. "This is a pleasant surprise, Elora," he said, but his expression quickly shifted to one of concern. "But you're not here on a social call."

She shook her head. "Ben's been kidnapped."

Thomas's eyes widened and he nearly dropped his cigarette.

"I was hoping you or Emmanuelle would know the vampire… society, I suppose, in London," she began. "I think I know who ordered Ben's kidnapping, but I don't know where they congregate."

"Emmanuelle's still awake," Thomas replied. "You're lucky. I wanted to have a cuppa and a coffin nail before I turned in, too. If you'd been ten minutes later, the dirigible would have been shut up for the day. Please excuse Emmanuelle for not coming out from below deck to speak with you."

"I understand completely," Elora said. Remembering her manners, she added, "This is Mr. Sloan. He has an interest in finding Ben, too."

She didn't have it in her to explain why a policeman was investigating vampires, and she hoped Sloan wouldn't correct her.

Fortunately, he picked up on her hint and didn't. "Pleasure to meet you," he said.

"Likewise," Thomas replied. "Come on up." Once they were aboard the dirigible, in the same glass-enclosed part of the deck, Thomas told them to wait while he went below to speak with Emmanuelle.

Elora's heart ached and her pulse raced, wondering what the vampire would tell her, if she would tell her anything. By her own admission, she hadn't spent much time in London since Angelique released her, decades ago.

She and Sergeant Sloan occasionally glanced at one another while they waited. Elora thought asking him if he'd ever actually met a vampire other than Ben, but refrained from it. Emmanuelle would hear her whisper. Elora checked her tarnished silver pocket watch and saw that it was only a little past six.

His wrists were bound with silver when he was taken. Dear God, she hoped his captors had removed them. She couldn't bite back a choked sob when she put away the watch.

"Miss Stone."

She looked at Sloan, who held out a handkerchief to her. Shaking her head, she removed her own from her skirt pocket and dabbed at her eyes. "Thank you, though," she said as he tucked his away.

A few moments later, Thomas's footsteps sounded on the stairs and he reappeared in the glass-enclosed lounge. "Elora, Emmanuelle wants to speak to you."

She followed him downstairs. "I'll be right back," she said over her shoulder to Sloan.

Lamps were lit down here, and the space had a surprisingly luxurious feel. Elora had been delighted with the below deck accommodations when Thomas gave her a tour the night before, how living in the sky seemed like the ultimate adventure. Now, she could already picture herself being sick before the dirigible's anchor was cast off. Flying was definitely not for her.

Emmanuelle stood in the middle of the room, wearing a silk dressing gown. Her long red hair was loose, and she looked almost angelic in the warm yellow light offered by the lamps. It was a sharp contrast to the room's decor, with its embroidered tapestries covering the walls that acted as a buffer against the engine's noise. It was filled with heavy dark wooden furniture overlaid with pillows, hand-stitched blankets, and furs. It looked the way Elora imagined a brothel must look like.

Emmanuelle surprised her when she enveloped Elora in a hug. "I'm so sorry," she whispered. "This is a tragedy."

"He's still alive," Elora said, tamping down her threatening hysteria. "He has to be. I just don't know where he could be held."

"I mean, it's a tragedy that he was taken," Emmanuelle corrected.

"Do you know of vampires called Denis or Louis?" Elora asked. She sniffled and wiped away a few more tears. "I think they were friends with Angelique."

Emmanuelle said something in a language Elora didn't recognize, but she guessed it was a curse. "The three of them were well acquainted. I wouldn't say friends, because Angelique had a sadistic side that was a little too intense for them at times. They were all turned around the time of the Reign of Terror."

"Oh," said Elora.

"I don't know who turned them or which faction they supported during the Revolution, but it doesn't matter and you're not here to listen to me tell you about how they would relive those days and nights during the times they were getting along." Emmanuelle held Elora's hands in her own, a cool and calming presence she needed right now. "They prefer the docks along the Thames. They used to set up their nest in an abandoned glass factory in Wapping. Kinley's Glassworks, I believe it was called. I would look there, and you'll need weapons. Holy water, if you can get it, and stakes. I'm sorry I can't tell you more. I haven't been to the factory in many years and I don't know if they still convene there."

Now, it was Elora's turn to throw her arms around Emmanuelle, wrapping her in a fierce hug. "Thank you," she said into her hair. "You don't know what this means to me."

"I would go to the end of the earth for Thomas," Emmanuelle replied, returning the hug. "He would do the same for me. We would kill for each other. We *have* killed for each other." She pulled away, her gaze searching Elora's face. "Are you prepared to do that?"

"I already have. I killed Denis the night we met."

Emmanuelle sighed and smiled. "This gives me faith that you can do this. I would go with you, but I can already sense the sun is rising."

"I'll go," Thomas volunteered.

"Absolutely not," said Elora, just as Emmanuelle said, "No."

"Mr. Sloan will help," Elora added.

"I heard him upstairs," Emmanuelle said. "I can smell him from here. He isn't a threat, but there's something different about him."

Elora nodded but didn't elaborate. It wasn't as if she could, anyway. Sergeant Merritt Sloan had a knack for showing up at the strangest times and had a preternatural ability to suss out vampires. She doubted Sloan would tell her what he was, if he possessed any supernatural traits.

"He isn't a were," Emmanuelle said. "Nor a dhampir. I'm damned if I can guess what he is." She looked up at the ceiling as if the policeman himself would come downstairs and announce what he was.

"But that isn't important," Emmanuelle continued. "Go to Kinley's Glassworks in Wapping. That's the best place to start looking."

CHAPTER 14

*B*en was frog-marched from the steam cab and held in place by the man, who still hadn't given him his name. From the sounds and smells of everything, they were near the river. They were likely in an alley that reeked of vermin and filth. He was almost grateful for the hood over his head that blocked out the worst of the stink, and he breathed quick, shallow breaths through his mouth.

"Damn it," Caroline cursed from a few feet away. Ben heard the clank of chain against metal, and then the scraping sound of rusted metal on rusted metal.

The man pulled on Ben's wrist chains, urging him forward. Ben didn't try to hide his agony at the movement. "You just have to ask," he said sharply. "I told you that you have my full cooperation provided my companion is unharmed."

The only response he received was a grunt.

Ben tried again. "How long have you been Louis's familiar?" That question earned him another tug on the silver chains. The resulting sizzle of burning flesh sounded much louder to his ears than it probably was, and he bit back a scream.

The air changed as they walked into what Ben assumed was a building. It was heavy and close, smelling thickly of mice, dust, and… he sniffed. Copper.

No, not copper. Blood.

It didn't smell like the kind of blood Ben dined on, but something else, more sinister. It smelled the way Ben imagined a human heart did. People were tortured here, vampires and humans alike.

The cowl and gloves were pulled off him in short, undignified movements, further jostling the chains. When Ben looked down at his hands, he had to bite back a yelp. The flesh around them was burned until it blackened and pieces of it had rubbed away, revealing viscera underneath. The silver itself was stained with blood.

It was so much worse than he thought it would be.

He tore his gaze away from his mangled skin and looked around. They stood in a massive room, its windows blacked out and boarded over, dimly lit with mismatching electric lights and gas lamps. What looked like gigantic ovens were installed along the far wall, the doors open to reveal cold ashes. Ben shuddered to think about what the ovens could be used for.

Regret raced through him as the man and Caroline flanked him on either side. They forced him to walk through the room. Regret for bringing Elora into this mess in the first place. For not meeting her when he was still human. For loving her when all he could bring her was pain and life on the perpetual run. Regret for not being a better man when he was still alive, for fucking around and taking his family for granted. He should have followed George's lead, taken an interest in the family business, and thus avoided being turned into a vampire in the first place.

He and Elora would have married, settled into a perfectly ordinary life with children of their own in an ordinary townhouse near his parents' home…

He was shoved forward and he fell to his knee and looked up in the face of an enraged Louis.

The old vampire sat on a velvet-covered chair in an alcove off the building's main floor, a marked, luxurious contrast to the bleakness of the rest of the place. "Sir," said the man reverently, and knelt at his feet beside Ben.

Louis nodded and placed a hand on his shoulder. "You've done well, Geoffrey." Looking at Caroline, he added, "And you as well."

Caroline wiped away tears. "Anything for Denis."

If the situation hadn't been so dire, Ben might have found it ridiculous. He was suddenly very glad that Elora had never fawned over him like this. It was definitely weird.

Louis turned to Ben, mouth contorted in anger. "You lying *fuck*."

In less than the blink of an eye, the older vampire had bodily picked up Ben and thrown him against the wall.

Something in his body crunched and snapped. The silver chains were pressed harder into his skin when he fell to the floor. He didn't try to muffle his scream this time. Nor did he deny killing Denis. Louis was determined to exact his revenge for the true death of his friend, and he would do everything he could to keep Elora safe from feeling the brunt of it.

He raised his head and saw Louis loom over him, face a mask of rage. His hands were now encased in black leather gloves, and he held a long silver chain in them, heavier than the ones around his wrists.

"You're going to have to beg me to kill you before I'll actually do it," Louis said, and he swung the chain.

Ben closed his eyes and waited for the blow to his

exposed skin. He wished he was anywhere but this stinking building. He thought he could feel his soul drifting away, and he wondered if Louis had just killed him instead, and he had stepped onto another plane. Not stepped. Floated. He was floating, a few feet off the floor. "What the hell?" he said aloud.

Louis stared at him, confused, as Ben's eyes met his and he floated upward.

God damn it, I think I figured out how to fly! He continued to picture himself floating, and he did so until he reached the ceiling.

Louis shook himself out of his stupor and immediately followed Ben in the air, the chain still in his hands.

Without overthinking his newfound ability to fly, Ben propelled his body forward, away from Louis, out of the alcove to the giant main room, picking up speed as he went. He willed himself upward, and he sailed toward the ceiling, at least thirty feet above the floor. Dusty catwalks were suspended from the ceiling, held in place by rusted supports. Ben didn't want to test their limits.

Louis was hot at his heels and snapped the chain at him a few times.

Ben's clothes deflected the blows, but he still felt the metal's brutal heat through the fabric.

Hope rose in him, bright as the sun on a summer day.

STAKES at the ready and with Sergeant Sloan's clockwork pistol loaded with silver bullets, Elora and Sloan stepped out of the ornithopter's basket. They had landed without a mishap on the roof of the abandoned Kinley's Glassworks. They easily found the building, tucked among a group of other derelict structures near Wapping's docks, and decided that the best way to infiltrate it was from the roof, for the element of surprise.

Elora hoped Emmanuelle was right, that Louis and Denis still used the factory as their hideout. It made perfect sense. The location meant there was ready access to sailors and transients for food, and it would be easy to dispose of drained bodies. She had spotted blacked-out and boarded-over windows all over the factory during their flight, which told her that there was a good chance Louis was inside. Some of the boards looked like they were recently replaced.

To their relief, there was an entrance to the building on the roof, a door inset in a small shed-like structure. Sergeant Sloan broke off the locks guarding it and urged it open on rusted hinges. He held a flameless candle into the shed, and Elora saw a spiral staircase leading down into the building. Sloan removed his clockwork pistol from its holster under his coat. "Stay behind me," he ordered. "Keep that stake ready."

Elora nodded and gripped the wooden stake a little more securely in her hand. She noted the outline of Sloan's under his coat, tucked in the back waistband of his trousers. They hadn't tried to find holy water, not wanting to waste any more time, and Elora hoped they wouldn't need it. Weapons at the ready, they tiptoed down the stairs, the metal occasionally groaning under their weight. There was no light to speak of aside from Sloan's candle and Elora found herself getting dizzy from the constant turning after a moment. She blinked and continued moving, until the stark illumination of electric light came into view.

Lights meant that someone was present.

The spiral staircase ended on what looked like an old factory floor, stripped bare for the giant furnaces that would have been used to melt and shape glass. Sloan motioned to Elora to follow him, and they hid behind one of the furnaces.

Not a moment later, the pair who kidnapped Ben ran to the floor, distraught. Both had their guns aimed at the ceiling.

What the hell is going on?

A scream rent the air. Elora and Sloan both looked up to see a pair of bodies tangling twenty or thirty feet above them in a vicious fight. A few drops of blood fell on the floor. With her heart in her throat, Elora recognized Ben's dark hair and clothes, and the pale-haired Louis, hands pulling on the silver chains that still bound Ben's wrists. She nearly cried out, but Sloan clapped his hand over her mouth just in time.

He shook his head. *Not now.*

The woman familiar fired off a shot at them. Ben fell to the floor, flat on his back, an agonized, inhuman scream escaping him. Louis gracefully landed on his feet next to him, his back to Elora and Sloan.

Elora thought she might be sick, or scream. *The bitch shot Ben!*

Sloan shook her arm and jerked his head to the three of them huddled around Ben. He cocked his gun and gave her a knowing look before inclining his head at the group. She realized he was telling her to rush at them, take them by surprise.

Galvanized by fury, she nodded.

In two swift movements, Sloan aimed and fired his clockwork pistol. Bullets struck the human woman in the back and the man next to her in the chest.

Louis whirled around and flew at them with a terrifying, inhuman speed Elora didn't expect. He knocked the stake out of her hand and Sloan and her to the floor. She landed with a hard thump on her back that knocked the wind out of her. She coughed, trying to get it back.

In a flash, Louis was suspended over her, floating in the air, fangs extended, eyes red with anger. He mumbled a curse in French and ripped at her disheveled hair, jerking it to pull her head to the side. His breath landed on her face and nausea roiled over her at the rotting flesh scent, the odor of death. It was going to be the last thing she ever smelled.

That was it for her.

Oh, Ben, I tried. I really did. She closed her eyes, unable to look her killer in the eye before he did it.

His body collapsed against hers and a garbled scream escaped his throat, blowing more death-scented breath into her face. She opened her eyes to see Louis, eyes wide open in shock. Blood and black gore issued from his mouth, covering her clothes. She tried to wiggle away, but he was too heavy.

Ben stood above him, his hand still on the stake in Louis's back. With a strength that looked like his last, his face contorted in pain, he forced the dying vampire off Elora's body, then fell to the floor in a dead faint.

Then everything was silent.

Elora didn't know how much time passed before Sloan helped her up. She stumbled in place and he held her arms to keep her from falling over. She shook him off and immediately crouched beside Ben. He had burn marks over his face the skin on his wrists were peeling. He looked sick. She shook his shoulders. "Ben, wake up."

He stirred a little, but his eyes didn't open.

"Miss Stone, we still have the matter of these bodies to attend to," Sloan said.

"We can handle them later."

"I would advise against delaying that. Someone may

have heard the gunshots. I doubt they hear a great deal of them at this time of day, even in Wapping."

Damn him, but the policeman was right. "How are we going to get rid of them in broad daylight?"

"We'll find a spot to hide them now and return at sundown to drop them in the river. But I think it's prudent for all of us to leave here as soon as possible."

"What about Ben?" she protested. His eyelids fluttered, an encouraging sign, but he hadn't woken up yet. "He'll need help getting out of here, and we have to cover him up. Can your ornithopter even handle three people?"

"It can fly up to four."

"It can barely hold two!"

"It can hold up to four, provided one of the passengers isn't clinging to the pilot for dear life," Sloan corrected her. With a sigh, he draped Louis's black cape over his rapidly decomposing face.

Elora looked down at her clothes, at the gore streaked across them. She gingerly touched her hair, and a piece of… something came off in her hand. A piece of bloody skin. Gagging, she flicked it away and rubbed her hand on her skirt before she remembered it was covered in pieces of Louis.

Ben stirred again and he opened his bloodshot eyes. They widened when they fixed on Elora. "My God," he whispered, and touched her hair. "You found me."

"You saved me," she whispered. "Louis was going to kill me."

"I've repaid your debt, in that case."

"I wasn't keeping score."

He tried to sit up but clearly lacked the strength. "I flew," he said, voice cracking. "I don't know how I did it, but I stayed alive long enough doing it."

"Don't try to fly right now," she urged him.

"I'm not. I just want to sit up and kiss you."

Sloan cleared his throat. "I'm going to see if there isn't something I can cover the bodies with," he announced and left the factory floor.

"They were Denis and Louis's familiars," Ben said. "Caroline and Geoffrey."

"Caroline shot you!"

"She did." Ben lifted his shirt to reveal the bloody, blackening wound. "She shot *at* me and I think it grazed me. The bullets were silver. If she'd actually shot me, I would be truly dead." In all his suffering, he tried to lift his eyebrow at her in jest.

"You need to heal." She unfastened the top buttons of her filthy blouse to reveal her neck. "You aren't strong enough to get back to the hotel right now."

"How did you get here?"

Bless him, he didn't argue with her about his need to eat right now. "On an ornithopter. The one flown by Sergeant Sloan, the policeman from Liverpool. He knows about vampires."

"I was wondering why he was here, but I was too focused on you and saving you," Ben said. Almost as an afterthought, he added, "Is he going to kill me?"

"No." Elora lay next to him, propped on her side with her neck exposed to make it easier for Ben to reach her. He had already sunk his fangs into her neck by the time Sloan returned with dirty horse blankets and rope piled in his arms. He nearly dropped them when he saw them on the floor. Elora could hardly blame him. It was an awkward thing to walk in on. "It's quite all right," she said.

Ben raised his head to look at the stunned policeman over his shoulder.

"I'll only be a moment," Sloan muttered and tossed

blankets over each of the human bodies. He tied ropes around them to secure them in place.

Ben's mouth again found the spot on Elora's neck where he fed from.

Sloan dragged away one of the bodies.

Ben lifted his head again and licked at her wound, healing the skin there. "That will keep me going until we get back to the hotel or wherever we spend the rest of the day, I don't mind." His voice was still rough but stronger, and when he lifted his shirt and cuffs to check on his wounds.

Elora could see they were already healing, but they had a while to go. At least the skin no longer looked burnt. "I thought we could spend the day at Thomas and Emmanuelle's dirigible. Emmanuelle was the one who suggested I come here to look for you. This used to be a glassworks factory. Angelique, Louis, and Denis used to convene here, according to her. Besides, the Vauxhall Airfield is closer to here than the hotel."

Ben threaded his fingers through hers. "I'll go anywhere you want to go."

"So, we'll go to the dirigible. Emmanuelle will better know how to help you heal."

"I have to tell you something," Ben said, just as Sloan returned.

"There's a door at the back that leads to the docks," the policeman announced. "Incredibly convenient for our purposes. I can see why vampires like this place. I've left one body beside the door and I'll haul the other there now. We'll return tonight to dispose of all of them. I saw a couple of people milling about the docks and I don't feel confident getting rid of them now." He gave a disgusted look at the pile of rotting viscera that used to be Louis.

Elora didn't miss how Sloan said 'we.' She was fine

with that. She would be forever indebted to Sloan for his help this morning.

Ben waited until Sloan dragged away the other body before he kissed Elora, a fierce, possessive gesture. "I love you and I have no business doing so. I can't provide you with the life you deserve. I'm the most selfish man I know and I will do anything to keep you with me." His words came out in a tumble, like he was afraid Louis would come back to life and stake him and he needed to let Elora know in case he didn't get another chance.

Or she walked away into the sunlight, leaving him behind in the abandoned factory.

"I want what Emmanuelle and Thomas have.," he continued. "I will marry you in a church if that's what you want, but I want us to be together forever. A blood bond will do that."

"Ben."

"She told me last night how it's done. We drink a little of each other's blood. You wouldn't be a vampire, but you'd live as long as I do."

"*Ben.*" Something in her tone made him stop and turn beseeching eyes to her.

She brushed a lock of dark hair off his forehead and pressed a kiss to his lips. "I love you, too," she murmured against his mouth. "I don't care about any of the things you think I deserve. I've never wanted that kind of life. I'll be your blood mate. I *want* to be and I'll be your wife. We promised your parents we would get married, after all."

He responded with a kiss that made her forget where they were, and when he pulled at the ruined collar of her blouse, the sound of Sloan clearing his throat again reminded her that there was still work to be done.

Both of them stood up on wobbly legs, for different reasons. "Can you take us back to the airfield?" she asked.

"We'll come back here tonight to help you get rid of the bodies."

"I found a spare blanket for Mr. Lang," Sloan replied. "Let's get away from this place."

It was a slow, careful climb up the spiral staircase to the roof, with Ben needing to take the occasional break to regain his strength. Shortly before they reached the top stairs, he draped the blanket over his head and let Elora hold it tight around him as they made the fastest beeline possible to the waiting ornithopter. He huddled on the basket's floor with the blanket tucked around him, while Sloan and Elora strapped on their flight goggles.

Even though Ben was safe as could be under the circumstances, Elora still held Sloan for dear life as the flying machine took off and tipped slightly to its side over Kinley's Glassworks's roof. Sloan righted the craft and it sped through London's skies as the city woke up.

THEY SPENT the daylight hours in a small room aboard Emmanuelle and Thomas's dirigible, the couple passing along advice to better help Ben heal while he occasionally fed from Elora between naps. Emmanuelle graciously offered Elora a change of clothes. She spent part of the afternoon on the dirigible's deck with Thomas and Sloan, who had his own questions about vampires.

She didn't know if Sloan let it slip that he was a policeman, and she suspected Thomas didn't care about that, anyway. She was curious about Emmanuelle's theory that he wasn't entirely human, but didn't dare ask. He had been kind to them, and he seemed to be conducting his work out of compassion. She also didn't want to know if there were others of his kind who weren't as goodhearted as Sloan was, as Ben and Emmanuelle were to vampires. She didn't need another supernatural being angry with her.

Elora, Sloan, and Ben returned to the glassworks factory under cover of darkness to dispose of the familiars' bodies and Louis's traces. They parted ways from there. Sloan took off in his ornithopter, and Elora and Ben took a steam cab back to The Savoy.

It was over, truly over. They could go anywhere they wanted. Finally, this was the fresh start both of them craved.

Once back at the hotel, Elora locked their door behind them and leaned against it, surveying the room. House-keeping had come by and made the bed, a pleasant surprise to come back to. "I never want to get rid of a body again," she said, a shudder rippling through her.

"You never will," Ben said. "I promise." He reached for her hands and held them in his, a contrast of cool and warm. He was still a man, Elora knew. Just in a different form. "I meant everything I said today." He stroked the backs of her hands with his thumbs. "I love you and I'm willing to fight for you."

"Fighting isn't necessary. I never want to see a fight ever again, either."

"Elora…"

"And I meant what I said, too." She let go of his hands to take his face in hers, memorizing his features. "I love you. I want us to be blood mates, if it means we'll be together."

He responded with a kiss, and he led her away from the door toward the bed.

"Will this hurt?"

He unfastened the clasp on the blouse she borrowed from Emmanuelle to replace her ruined clothes, an imper-meable garment meant for dirigible flight. He pressed a kiss to the spot that still bore marks from his fangs from earlier. "No."

Elora wasn't sure if getting undressed was part of the ritual, and she didn't care. Ben removed his shirt, revealing pink skin where he was healing from his gunshot and silver chains. Concern immediately flared in her. "Does any of this hurt?"

"Not anymore, thanks to you."

She felt herself flush at the memories of Ben's feeding from her throughout the day. Once he stopped being in agony, both of them had been able to enjoy it but didn't want to get carried away in their hosts' home. Elora was unsure of the etiquette surrounding their situation but felt it best to err on the side of caution.

Ben tugged on her skirt. "Take this off," he ordered hoarsely.

She was only too happy to oblige.

"The shower's big enough for the two of us," he said, surprising her. "I still feel grimy from today."

So did Elora, for that matter. She had tried to clean up as best she could aboard the dirigible. But she needed more time in hot water and more soap. She touched her hair and cringed.

Ben took her hand and led her to the bathroom, turning on the levers that activated the shower system.

It was a convenient feature, Elora thought as she stripped out of the rest of her clothes. If she ever made it to the cottage, she'd dreamed about, she would have such a thing installed.

Ben had already shed the rest of his clothing, and he pulled her in under the pair of giant brass showerheads once the rushing water was warm enough. He scrubbed her hair for her, washing away the gore that streaked it, his fingers massaging her scalp. The aches and pains that inevitably resulted from being tossed around a glassworks factory by a vampire faded a little under the hot water. She sighed, leaning against Ben as the water rushed over them. "Where do you want to go?" she asked.

"I don't care. Perhaps we could travel for a spell, as I told my parents we would."

Elora took the soap from him and worked up some suds across his chest. "Do you mean we should make the lies we told your parents into truths, and go to Italy?"

"I'd prefer that you didn't mention my parents right now, but I'd love to go to Italy with you or anywhere. Italy has enough night time activity so we would have things to do."

"That sounds lovely."

Ben took the soap back from her and turned her around, stroking her back with it. He tucked her hair to the side and tilted her head. Excitement thrummed through her.

"Are you going to bite me?"

"If you want me to."

She craned her neck to look over her shoulder at him. "Did you want to do the blood bond?"

His eyes darkened and fangs extended. "Now?"

She nodded. "Yes."

"Are you certain?" he asked. "It's permanent."

"I told you already that I love you. I want to do this."

He responded by biting his forearm and held it out to her, bright pinpricks of blood that nearly washed away under the shower's water. "Drink," he commanded.

Heart pounding, she did so. She tried not to think about what she was doing exactly, knowing that it was a strange reaction to have when Ben regularly fed from her. She didn't stop until he pulled his arm away. He pushed her against the shower's tiles, eyes nearly black with lust, and bit into her throat.

This sensation was totally different, a welcome change, and a curious thrum traced through her, a feeling of magnetic pull toward Ben she hadn't felt before. He moaned against her as he fed, the sound reverberating in her body from his, pressed against her, his arousal pushed against her hip.

He lifted his head, fangs still extended.

The magnetic pull didn't fully abate, but shifted into something warm. A connection she could almost physically feel, and judging from the wide-eyed expression on his face, he did, too.

"I think we did it," he said.

Delight and relief, the promise of a long life ahead of her with the man she loved, had her looping her hands around his neck and pulling him toward her for a kiss. "I think we did, too," she murmured against his lips.

It wasn't until the water ran cold that they got out of the shower, and returned to bed.

EPILOGUE

*F**our months later*

Rome's evenings were still fairly warm, but there was a change in the air, a shift that autumn was about to befall the city. Elora could discern the chill before it landed, the way summer breezes were giving way to winds whose temperatures dropped a little more every night. She was looking forward to experiencing the seasons as Italy presented them.

She and Ben had originally planned to only stay in Italy for a couple of weeks. But Elora had fallen in love with Rome shortly after they arrived, and so they stayed. They rented a flat in a building that felt older than Rome itself, its indoor plumbing the only nod to modern conveniences. Elora didn't mind; for one thing, the small, narrow windows with their blurry panes of glass were easier to cover against the sun.

She didn't miss the daylight much. She could go out for a stroll in the sunshine, but she preferred to sleep the day away next to Ben and explore the city with him by night. They went to every art gallery and museum they could.

They stopped at tiny restaurants with only a couple of items on the menu, where Elora enjoyed food that didn't exist in England and Ben a glass of wine.

Since they were blood bonded, he could even eat small morsels of food on occasion.

For Elora, the blood bond meant her senses were sharper, more acute. They still weren't on par with Ben's, nor could she fly or move ten feet in less than a second, but she was still grateful for her newly granted abilities. They made life so much more interesting.

This evening, they strolled hand in hand through Rome's streets, still full of people past ten in the evening who nearly glowed under the gas-powered street lamps that appeared every twenty feet or so. Abruptly, Ben stopped in front of a massive fountain, water streaming from its top into a pool. "Sit down here," he said and pointed to the elevated edge of the pool.

A light spray misted her when she did so. "What's the occasion?"

"This is the Fontana della Barcaccia." He sounded nervous, uncharacteristic for him.

"It's beautiful," she said, looking over her shoulder at the water. Behind her, a stone staircase ascended higher than she had seen so far in Italy, or possibly anywhere. At the top was a magnificent light-colored building with a pair of bell towers that could only be a church.

"I can't believe we haven't been here yet," he said, and took a seat next to Elora.

"We've seen a lot of fountains on this journey."

"This one is in front of the Spanish Steps but there are too many pilgrims there right now … for us to be there, too."

The Spanish Steps sounded familiar. Elora racked her brain, trying to recall when she last discussed them, and suddenly remembered the conversation over supper with Ben's parents. How they met, how he proposed to her in front of the Spanish Steps.

"Oh, my God," she said.

Ben got up and kneeled in front of her, removing something from his coat pocket. A ring.

Shock had her unable to move for a few seconds. The sounds of Rome's nightlife and the water splashing behind her faded away. Once again, they were the only people in the world, and he was waiting for an answer to a question he hadn't asked yet. She already knew it. "Yes."

"Elora Stone, will you do me the honor…"

"I already said yes."

"I still want to ask. I'm never going to have to ask this question again, and I had it all planned out. Elora, will you marry me?" As an afterthought, he whispered, "The human way?"

"Yes," she said again.

Ben rose to his feet and slipped the ring on her left hand. When she lifted it to inspect it, a pearl winked at her, bright as a star in its simple gold setting. She couldn't have picked a nicer ring herself. Someone nearby clapped when she threw her arms around him and kissed him, but she didn't care. "I can't believe you remembered," she said, turning to look behind her at the Spanish Steps. As Ben said, people milled around on them.

"I couldn't think of a better way to do this. Although I confess it didn't occur to me until we decided to stay for the winter. I thought we could get married here and return to England in the spring, if you like. Or continue traveling. I don't have a preference, as long as I'm with you."

"We have time to decide," Elora said, beaming up at him. "All the time in the world."

1 December 1888

DEAR PETER,

I considered the advice you imparted on me in your final letter dated this past spring, and wanted to pass on the details that I am very happily married. Ben and I are looking forward to our first Christmas season together in Rome.

This is my final letter to you, as well. While I'm certain you don't care a whit about my wellbeing either way, a part of me did want to let you know that I'm the happiest I've ever been and will be until the end of my days.

I don't hate you, Peter, even though I doubt anyone would blame me if I did. I don't have the capacity to hate my fellow humans anymore. I do hope you find even a smidgen of the happiness I have found myself in.

Your sister,

Elora Lang

ABOUT THE AUTHOR

Jessica Marting is a sci-fi and paranormal romance author, art enthusiast (not quite an artist, despite all that time in art school), an avid reader, and makeup collector. She lives in Toronto.

www.ingramcontent.com/pod-product-compliance
Lightning Source LLC
Chambersburg PA
CBHW060921180626
46817CB00004B/1339